*Issue 18 — October 2023*
*https://australasianhorror.com/midnight-echo/*

I0584530

Like us on Facebook
Follow us on Twitter

Produced in Australia

AHWA

# ACKNOWLEDGEMENTS

Production Team:

Guest Editor

J. S. Bruekelaar

Executive Editor

Alan Baxter

Cover Art

Meg Wright

Layout

Greg Chapman

Proofreaders

Paul Sheldon

Claire Fitzpatrick

The Staff Would Like to Thank

*Midnight Echo*'s fantastic contributors, readers, and fans.

# CONTENTS

*††AHWA Short Story Competition Winner 2022*
*†††AHWA Flash Fiction Competition Winner 2022*
*‡ AsylumFest Ghost Story Competition Winner 2022*

## A WORD FROM THE PRESIDENT

You hold in your hands Midnight Echo 18: Cursed, and what a wonderful thing it is. J. S. Breukelaar has done a stellar job with this one, I know you're going to enjoy it. It's a bittersweet issue for me, as it's my last as President of the AHWA. I'll be stepping down right around the time this issue sees publication. It's been a privilege and an honour to serve as the AHWA's president these last three years, but it takes a lot of mental energy and it's a volunteer position, so I need to let someone else take over while I focus more on my own writing career. At this stage I'll be staying on as executive editor of Midnight Echo in the short term, but that's a largely invisible role because we always get such amazing editors on board.

In my time as president we've seen Midnight Echo return to a print publication as well as ebook, and we've seen the pay rate rise significantly. I'd still like to see that rise a lot higher, but the magazine is paid for by member fees from a non-profit Association, so there's only so much we can manage there. Regardless, I'm proud of where it stands.

I have a huge soft spot for this publication. I've been published in it myself several times before taking over, it's given people their first publications, it's won awards and the stories in it have won awards. Midnight Echo really does an amazing job of showcasing Australasian dark fiction, poetry and non-fiction, and long may it continue. Here's to many more.

Now, go and get yourself cursed.

**Alan Baxter, NSW,  October 2023**

# EDITORIAL

Our understanding of curses is deep. In our bones, and our blood, and our brains. Curses can be read as a dead metaphor and cost us no more than a coin pushed sheepishly into a swear jar, or as a monthly 'punishment' for being a woman, or as an easy plot device. But in their original form they are primal and terrible—the attachment of evil or misfortune to a person, or to a family or a place, that is inescapable, undeserved, fatal.

Curses are power. Curses take on a life of their own. They are the ultimate weapon because the harm they inflict comes from an abyssal place—the wielder of curses has less mastery over their own powers than they think. In every sense, the curser is already cursed.

Curses are inhuman. They are pure spite. Curses play God. They defy the golden rule to forgive that we may be forgiven. Do unto others? Forget it. Curses are the work of an Other devoid of compassion, of conscience, a stranger, forever, to kindness.

Curses cross a line. They turn homes into hells. Lives into death. Innocence into corruption. Free will into dread.

Curses are fun. And funny. They can give a king the ears of a donkey, turn princesses into ogres, aristos into grovelling beasts. They can bring down mean girls and show bad boyfriends a thing or two. At their best and most hopeful, curses can transform.

In this issue, authors established and emerging explode the idea of traditional curses. In the fallout we see post-colonial vampires, burnt-out rock wannabes, bored housewives, ghostly schoolchildren, rejected writers, cursed mums, dead-beat dads, and so much more. Pacts made on dark antipodean streets and in airplanes and in music studios, on the battlefield, by the sea, and in the bush. The age-old curses of loneliness, illness, failure, isolation, violence, self-loathing, and love. Above all, love.

Pushing, biting, tearing at the timeworn boundaries of fictional curses, Midnight Echo 18 has body horror, cosmic terrors, twisted fairy tales and oh so much weirdness. It has funny. Darkly, disturbingly, memorably funny.

Thank you to Alan Baxter and the AHWA, for drawing me into this pact. Thanks to Meg Wright for the bewitching cover art and Greg Chapman for his design magic. Congratulations to competition winners, Kaaron Warren, Leanbh Pearson, and Joseph Townsend for stories that are eerily on-theme.

And now it's me who's cursed. I can't get some of these stories out of my mind, my heart, my soul. And neither will you. That's the thing about storytelling. In the pact between reader and writer, between invention and reinvention, beneath and beyond the page—we all get more than we bargain for. In the hands of writers and artists like these, curses can be a blessing too.

**J.S. Breukelaar, Guest Editor, Midnight Echo Issue 18**
**October, 2023**

# CURSES: FACT OR FICTION— AUSTRALIA, NEW ZEALAND AND BEYOND

## BY CLAIRE FITZPATRICK

You are seated at a table within a tavern, somewhere in northwest Greece, second-century BCE. The tavern is dark, with hushed conversations slipping in and out of the rambunctious crowd. You are alone, enjoying your solitude, when a hooded figure comes along, pockets filled with magic stones, fortune-telling cards, and ancient scrolls with indecipherable script. He stands nearby, whispering about the power he possesses, and all the unimaginable things he can offer.
The barkeep overhears the conversation and orders two burley men to kick the unwelcome stranger out; all this talk hinders drinking. He's not selling as much beer and wine as he should. Before he is thrown from the tavern, the hooded figure curses the tavern and everyone inside. Weeks pass, and one by one, calamity befalls all who were within the tavern that night.

You notice a pattern of 'accidents.' First, a farmer loses his entire crop. Then a father loses his children to a house fire. A young man is thrown from a horse, killed by a broken neck. The barmaid gives birth to a stillborn child. These things are brushed aside as bad luck, but then you recall the hooded stranger. Not one to believe in such nonsense, you can't shake the uncomfortable feeling coiled tightly in your stomach. Could there be some truth to his proclamation? Maybe…just maybe…

For as long as humans have told stories, we've spoken of curses. In a cave, around a campfire, in a candle-lit house, often in hushed tones. From punishments to allegorical, plain bad luck to revenge, unexplained occurrences to uncanny coincidences—curses give explanations to the strange and unusual. Our misfortunes are often easier to understand when attributed to omniscient beings pulling the strings. Call it fate or religion, they are usually explained by something beyond human comprehension.

According to the Latin Dictionary, the word 'accursed' comes from the Latin term 'sacer', which is, incidentally, also the etymological root for the word 'sacred.' While the efficacy of curses derived, in part, from a belief in the power of both the written and spoken word, curses have come in various shapes and forms, including spells, effigies, and even the 'evil eye.'

Despite our knowledge of science, curses remain so popular in fiction, as many people are superstitious enough to believe them. It's hard to find someone who hasn't warned against breaking mirrors or standing under ladders. So, in the age of science and reason, why do some people genuinely believe in curses? Why do we delight in telling tales like the stranger in the tavern? And what can curses teach us about society?

Fiction often uses curses to teach people a lesson. *Horns* by Joe Hill deals with themes of grief, loss, obsession, love, and the supernatural through what can only be described as a curse. A year after his girlfriend's murder, Ignatius 'Ig' Perrish wakes up one day to find he has grown a pair of horns. However, these are no ordinary horns—they compel people to confess their sins and tell him about their deepest, darkest secrets. Ig's power is a curse he struggles to come to terms with— everyone believes he's the murderer. For why else would he grow a terrifying pair of horns? Hill uses the idea of curses against judging others based on their appearance. For it doesn't matter what we look like— evildoers often hide in plain sight.

The idea of a curse or a magically cursed object is not something one readily accepts as fact. However, oracles, curses, and superstitions were ordinary practices of people in the ancient world. Kings and queens had spiritual advisors who consulted with oracles to learn of their fate. With modernity came the Age of Reason, and scientifically proven answers to many questions. Sightings of ghosts and ghouls can usually be explained by logical phenomena. Continuous bad luck is attributed to a series of unconnected occurrences, explained away by quantifiable patterns within society. According to the 2002 study "Voodoo's role in Haitian mental health" by E. August, published in the American Journal of Psychotherapy, many clinicians within the field of psychiatry regard Haitian voodoo practitioners as mentally ill. Yet people often cling to the unknown when faced with a crisis of faith. *I have done nothing to deserve the loss of my entire family in a car accident. Surely there is some higher being or supernatural power inflicting harm upon me?*

Curses found throughout history provide a unique and rich snapshot of the culture of the ancient world. For example, curses on scrolls and tablets found in temples, dug up from graves, or left in long-abandoned villages give us insight into the cultural practices and beliefs of that time. Often, these texts appear to be written by ordinary citizens appealing to the gods and oracles to take away their pain— farmers, doctors, shopkeepers, and public officials, vengeful directives to the spirits from wives whose husbands have deserted them. Lust, jealousy, fear, and envy— there is a curse catering to every human experience.

One could say an accursed object is so sacred as to be rendered untouchable. *The Amulet* by Michael McDowell tells the story of the tragedies that befall various people in a small town after coming in possession of a cursed supernatural amulet. After a rifle range accident leaves her husband Dean in a vegetative state, Sarah finds herself burdened not only with the task of caring for him but enduring her hateful, overbearing mother-in-law, Jo. The woman blames the entire town for her son's accident and gives a strange amulet to the man she believed most responsible. As the cursed object makes its way across the town, one by one, everyone dies in horrific 'accidents.' The rich, the poor, the opinionated, the lost; anyone possessing the amulet is doomed to experience a horrible death. Seducing people with an explained evil allure that makes people want to possess it, no one is immune. McDowell explores the idea of everyone and no one being responsible, and collective guilt shared through possession, something existing within curses throughout history.

Many cursed-object stories stem from legends arising around the world's most 'cursed' jewels. For example, the Black Prince's Ruby (actually a 170-carat cabochon spinel), thought to have been mined in the mountains of Afghanistan, first appeared in the 14th century when the aptly named Don Pedro the Cruel, of Seville, Spain, stabbed Abu Sa'id to death (the Moorish Prince of Granada) and ransacked his corpse, stealing the red stone. But this act came with dire consequences; anyone possessing the stone was cursed to experience bad luck and eventual death. Of course, it's unlikely this particular gem inspired McDowell, but the idea of cursed jewellery is a story told throughout the ages as a way to ward off thieves. Planning to steal something that doesn't belong to you? Be prepared to face the consequences.

Curses within families often feature in horror fiction. *Seed* by Ania Ahlborn features a familiar curse running through Jack Winter's family. First experiencing it as a child, it returns following a car accident caused by a very familiar shadow Jack Winter sees on the road. In the car was his wife Aimee and their two daughters. Over time, things go awry, and Jack soon realises a demonic presence has taken over their home, slowly possessing their daughter Charlie. This is a different type of curse, as it focuses on inherited evil passing down through generations. Jack

watches his daughter experience the same evil he did and is helpless to do anything about it.

Familial or generational curses are prominent in horror fiction, passing down from parent to child, usually until the entire family line dies out (and the curse with it), or unless they find some way to break the curse. Usually, it occurs after being specifically placed upon the family by someone else, however, sometimes it can be the result of bad karma or black magic performed by an originating family member.

There are many famous familial curses throughout history. Legend says the Grimaldi family was cursed by a witch. Once one of the most powerful families in Genoa (eventually becoming lords of Monaco in the 15th century), it has been said that following an assault committed by Lord Rainier I in the 13th century, a young girl gained knowledge of the 'dark arts' to curse the entire family, ensuring no Grimaldi would ever find happiness in marriage.

Though initially brushed off, many calamities befell the family over the years, all relating to relationships and marriage. Most recently and perhaps famously, actress Grace Kelly, who left acting to marry Prince Rainer III, was killed in a car crash in 1982. Her daughter Stephanie, who survived the incident, endured one failed marriage and several other failed relationships later in life. Grace's other daughter, Caroline, also had a tumultuous love life, experiencing an early divorce, a second husband who died in a speedboat accident, and a third husband- a prince - with a reputation for aggression and unspecified medical problems. Princess

Grace's in-laws, Count Pierre de Polignac and Princess Charlotte are also said to have had an unhappy marriage, as were several other members of the royal family. Fact or fiction? While no one can prove the Grimaldi family was cursed, it's certainly fodder for many fictitious stories of generational curses.

Many books themselves are said to be cursed and deemed a threat to mankind. Society has used books to share knowledge and secrets with others and succeeding generations since time immemorial. Some claim to have relations to otherworldly dimensions, others with supernatural forces. *The Grand Grimoire* is considered one of the darkest books in the world, filled with black magic and knowledge on how to call on demons (including Lucifer's right-hand man, Lucifugé Rofocale) to make a deal with the devil. Believed to be written in 1521, different editions date the book to 1521, 1522 or 1421, however, it was likely written during the early 19th century. In his 1898 text *The Book of Black Magic and Pacts*, British occultist and scholar Arthur Edward Waite called the Grand Grimoire one of "the four specific and undisguised handbooks of Black Magic."

Divided into two books, the introductory chapter is attributed to somebody named Antonio Venitiana del Rabina, who supposedly gathered his information from the original writings of King Solomon. The book also describes several other demons (as well as the rituals to summon them) and many spells to conjure 'everyday' wants or desires, such as talking to spirits, being loved by a girl, making oneself invisible, and even winning a lottery. Now locked within Vatican City, the book has undergone many biblical rituals to ensure its negativity doesn't harm anyone.

*The Codex Gigas* is named one of the most mysterious books in the world. Also known as the Devil's Bible, it was written in the 13th century by a Buddhist monk at the Benedictine monastery of Podlažice in Bohemia, now a region in the modern-day Czech Republic. Eventually discovered in the imperial library of Rudolf II in Prague, the entire collection was stolen by the Swedish army in 1648 during the Thirty Years' War. Today, the manuscript is preserved and on display for the public at the National Library of Sweden in Stockholm.

According to legend, the monk broke his monastic vows and was sentenced to be walled up alive. To avoid this penalty, he promised to create, in one single night, a book to glorify the monastery forever, including all human knowledge. Fearing he would not be able to complete it, he called upon the fallen angel Lucifer, asking him to finish the book in exchange for his soul. Today, in tests to recreate the work, scientists have discovered that reproducing only the calligraphy, without any illustrations or embellishments, would have taken twenty years of non-stop writing, something unimaginable by a single person, let alone a monk in the 13th century.

Stories and legends claim the codex is cursed, bringing disaster or illness to whoever possesses it. Fortunately, the National Library appears immune to such a curse. However, the idea of a single person penning such a mammoth tome without the influence of a curse or spell is intriguing.

While many may laugh at the idea

of modern-day curses, some cultures vehemently believe in them and their power. According to the 2018 ABC news article by Emily Smith, *"Curses, black magic and witchdoctors: Ancient beliefs at large in remote NT communities"*, in Australia, ancient beliefs, legends, and curses continue to play a major part in many indigenous communities. For example, on Groote Eylandt, in the Gulf of Carpentaria, Indigenous residents widely believe in curses with the ability to be placed on any person, place, or object.

According to the 2004 Sydney Morning Herald news article *"PM Shrugs off Aboriginal Curse"*, an Aboriginal woman, backed by ousted Aboriginal and Torres Strait Islander Commission head Geoff Clark, put a supposed curse on then-Prime Minister John Howard in regional Victoria. This occurred a week after the prime minister scrapped the ATSIC, the peak Aboriginal organisation in the marginal Victorian seat of Corangamite. Clad in possum skin, the woman, known only as Moopar, pointed a small bone at Mr Howard as he got into his car following a speaking event in front of more than 500 members of the local community. While the prime minister seemed nonchalant about the curse, Clark told the media the cursed Mr Howard had a choice to either let Aboriginal people take control of their affairs or be cursed until the federal election. While we know John Howard served as prime minister until 2007, a curse is still a curse.

Years later, in 2018, a supposed curse was inflicted on both the Angurugu School and the local human services office, forcing both to close for thirteen days. According to another ABC article by

Emily Smith, *"Remote NT school reopens after Indigenous ceremony removes 'curse'"*, the lifting of the curse was eventually done through a smoking ceremony, conducted from the Anindilyakwa Land Council-administered royalty entitlements of the people who placed the curse.

Many curses are performed publicly to ensure everyone is aware of their existence, delivered through song, spoken by the person, or by pointing to something, like a bone. This ritual is believed to draw a malevolent force out of the spiritual dimension to be placed on an object or person (in the case above, the Angurugu School and the local human services office). Pointing bones have been used as a method of 'execution' by indigenous people for centuries, made by either human, kangaroo, or emu bone, and sometimes wood.

One of the most well-known curses in Australia is the 'Uluru Curse.' While there is no known curse that the Anangu (the traditional custodians of the area) are aware of, they acknowledge removing rocks from the area is hugely disrespectful to their beliefs and culture. However, many stories in recent history describe tourists experiencing strings of bad luck, as reported in the 2018 New Zealand Herald article *"Uluru tourists return 'cursed' souvenirs"* by Kathy Marks. Personal tragedies, or accidents, after pocketing a small piece of the famous rock. The Anangu custodians receive a parcel of returned rocks, seeds, twigs, sand, or pebbles almost every single day. There have been so many rocks returned with accompanying stories of bad luck they're officially known as the 'Sorry Rocks.' Of course, one can assume these unfortunate occurrences are purely coincidental, blamed on the rocks out of guilt. However, it is interesting to think of bad karma as a curse.

In New Zealand (Aotearoa), traditional Māori culture has similar curses. The makutu, which many Māori believe are deliberately placed curses to harm people, has been linked to several deaths. The word itself means 'witchcraft', 'sorcery', or 'to bewitch' in the Māori language. The 2009 New Zealand Herald article *"Five Guilty of Exorcism Case"*, reports that in 2007 a young mother drowned in a pool, with a subsequent investigation suggesting a curse surrounding a stolen object was the cause of her illness and eventual drowning. The investigation also uncovered a ceremony involving so much water that the carpet was saturated, and floorboards became dangerous to walk on. According to Māori belief, water and a simple *karakia* or prayer are used to cleanse a person by submerging him or her in water. It is, of course, unknown if the ceremony and the drowning are connected, however, it's interesting to note such a belief remains widespread within Māori culture.

Curses of objects, families, books, and places remain entrenched within society, continuing to inspire fiction. And how could they not? Curses can burden a character, predict future events, and contribute to interesting timelines and family trees. They form myths and superstitions about society and can shape both the collective identity of a family and the individual identities of its members. To ensure the curse maintains immense power throughout generations, they're usually hard to break, often requiring an extensive investigation, a long journey (mentally and/or physically), and challenging obstacles finally end it. They are the perfect premise for a story about a dark and mysterious stranger in a tavern, telling macabre tales about mysterious accidents and strange calamities that can't possibly be coincidence.

So why do we still believe in them?

Modern science dismisses the notion of curses, yet they continue to prevail. While a rational mind may concede a curse as nothing more than a self-fulfilling prophecy, engendered and sustained by cultural and shared beliefs, others, for various personal or cultural reasons, may not agree. One must keep in mind the idea of curses came before the Age of Reason, when societies lacked a comprehensive scientific understanding of the world in which they lived. A lightning flash was attributed to a god throwing a sword. Deep-sea fishermen survived torrential storms due to the deities they called upon to save them. Today, curses need not be real to be effective. Even if one doesn't consciously believe in them, they may still maintain superstitious beliefs, such as avoiding walking under ladders or keeping a rabbit's foot for good luck. Ideas of curses can be implanted, eschewing personal responsibility for events beyond our comprehension.

Maybe we believe in curses because we're fundamentally flawed. Did everyone see Ig Perrish as a monster because society expected him to be one? Can inherent evil be passed along through generations of families like Jack Winter's? Or is it stubbornness or unwillingness to change that continues the 'curse'? Is everyone or no one responsible for accidents and collective guilt?

Of course, those with an internal locus of control are few and far between. While our rational mind may be saying, 'Don't be silly and superstitious,' our subconscious mind is unable to verify, beyond a shadow of a doubt, that something isn't true. There are some things we simply cannot know (and some things better left unknown). Of course, many of us will outwardly doubt the power of curses, but some will inwardly worry that maybe, just maybe, they may contain an inkling of truth.

That mysterious man in the tavern? There might be something to his tall tale after all.

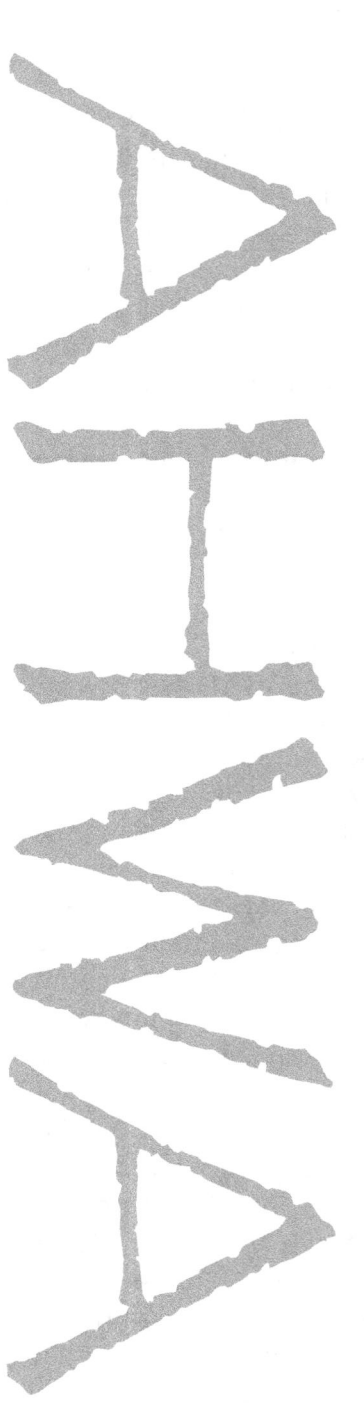

# THE THINGS SHE CARRIED

## BY N. KING

She was washing the blood from her fingertips as he walked into the bathroom, little rivulets of red running down the side of the basin. He came up behind her and wrapped an arm around her waist, splaying his fingers across her belly. Watching him in the mirror, she could see the moment he caught sight of the tampon wrapper on the counter—a frown washed over his face and his body shrank infinitesimally away from hers, the tiniest of spaces opening up between them. They had been doing this dance for months, his frown growing more pronounced each time, she carefully avoiding her own reflection, unsure of what she would see, perhaps sorrow or failure or fear … perhaps relief that she was not yet forced to sacrifice all that she was or might be in order to become everything to someone else.

When she left the house, he would call his mother who would be ready with fertility advice and remonstrations and old folk remedies that ranged from laughable to nauseating and on one narrowly avoided occasion, potentially deadly. His mother had always been kind but viewed her daughter-in-law's body through avaricious eyes, and as the months passed, the older woman's helpfulness carried a growing undercurrent of silent censure.

Through the window she could see the yellow leaves blowing in the wind, flying up to the tops of the buildings, tumbling over as they swirled together, weightless, seemingly never to return to the ground. She pulled on her thick coat and looked back over her shoulder,

"Please, will you pass me my bag?"

He picked up the well-worn leather bag and passed it across to her. "Oof, it's so heavy, what on earth do you have in there? You carry too much, surely you don't need all this."

She smiled tightly as she shouldered the bag and stepped out into the wind, leaves immediately catching in her hair. The bright flashes of yellow cheered her and she stopped for a moment to watch them in their dance. The bag was heavy, he was right. Each night she lay in bed cataloguing the aches in her body—the stiff neck, sore shoulders, aching hips, from the weight of the burden she carried each day.

As she walked toward the bus stop, she felt around in the bag, identifying the different objects by touch. A cold metal cylinder, lipstick, to redden her lips. The pert young woman who sold it to her had told her it had a blue undertone, to make her teeth whiter. To give her the teeth of someone who never drank a coffee or had a glass of red wine. And every time she did have a cup of coffee or a glass of wine, she had to run to a mirror to reapply and maintain the illusion of perfect lips. She pulled the lipstick out of the bag and threw it into the bin as she walked past. She had agonised over that purchase: it had cost her sixty-seven dollars.

She fished through her bag again and again, discarding the mascara that made her lashes longer and blacker, the bronzer that made her skin browner, the blush that made it pinker, the highlighter that made it look dewy and the powder that made it look matte. Hundreds of dollars worth of shiny containers, discarded like a little breadcrumb trail between her home and the bus stop.

She boarded the bus and, taking a tissue from the cavernous bag, she wiped the red glaze from her mouth. She felt her lips curve, unbidden, into a grin. Across the aisle, a man grinned back at her, "You're a cheerful one!"

Her mouth sank a little, the moderated smile. The one that said, I'm not being rude, but I'm not encouraging you either. The platonic, friendly, but not too friendly, *not like that*, smile. The *I want to believe you're just being nice but experience has taught me otherwise* smile.

She searched for an innocuous comment, "It's such a beautiful day," she said, gesturing to the blue sky and the autumn-painted leaves that hung in the trees and brushed occasionally at the bus windows. The man's grin broadened and he shifted in his seat as though about to get up and sit beside her. Quickly she hefted her bag up from the floor to plant it on the empty place. It was still very heavy.

She pulled her phone from her pocket and looked at it enquiringly, as though it had just rung. Then she held it to her ear, "Hello darling," she cooed into the silent phone. From a few seats ahead of her, another woman turned her head and briefly their eyes caught, a moment of understanding, of solidarity. In a second it was gone, she was alone again, with her heavy bag and her imaginary phone call.

She wished her pretend caller goodbye, fished out her headphones and ostentatiously placed them into her ears, sinking into a quiet cocoon and relegating the bus and her fellow passengers to the background. Increasingly, this was how she spent her time, hearing the world with the volume turned down, an isolated observer. The bus reached her stop and she disembarked, beginning the familiar walk up the hill along the side of the station to the entrance, taking long strides in her trainers. But she felt her shoulders begin to ache already. She paused and felt around in her bag, pulling out the black stilettos that she would don once she reached her client's office. The narrow pointed toes that pinched at her feet and the tall, spiked heels that required her to carefully measure each step across a marble-tiled lobby, a staircase, an escalator, paving stones, grates. All of them obstacles which required careful navigation. She stopped for a moment, weighing the shiny black shoes in her hand, and then casually tossed them down over the metal railing. They landed on the street below, gloss-bright against the dull grey of the tarmac. She remembered when it had felt like an achievement to wear those shoes, and stride through the streets on their spindly heels. Now she turned away and left them behind as their red soles winked up at her reproachfully.

She was lucky enough to find a seat on

the train, crammed in next to the window. She spent the journey pulling pieces of paper from her bag, folding them into tiny slivers and surreptitiously jamming them into the space between the seat and the carriage wall. When she finally exited the train, she left behind the to-do lists, and reminders and little scraps of paper on which she had scribbled the items that others thought it important she remember. She left the receipts that told the story of a life lived in motion at the service of others, the takeaway coffee, the pre-packaged sandwich, the breakfast roll eaten at 7pm, the consolation chocolate bar purchased for the late-night train ride home. She did not look back.

As she walked down the platform, her phone vibrated in her hand, the screen lit up with reminders of meetings, tasks, email and texts all waiting for answers. She stopped briefly, staring down at the little device that contained and controlled so much of her life, unheeding of the tuts and annoyed glances of the other passengers as they navigated around her. Then she walked slowly over to the edge of the platform and dropped the phone onto the tracks. A trio of teenagers shrieked and pointed at her, another got out their own phone and started filming, but she ignored them and walked on. The charging cable and spare battery were discarded at the ticket barrier and as she strode across the concourse she felt a swell of relief at having silenced the frenetic, anxious buzzing of the thousand tiny voices her phone had housed, all shouting their demands through a series of incessant pings and beeps and endless vibrations.

She emerged into the bustling street and was jostled between her fellow commuters, so many grey-suited shoulders and oversized briefcases. They marched like an army, down the street, across the bridge toward the city. But this morning, she was out of sync and she began to feel that each shoulder knocked her back a step until she was being pushed against the current; each step forward became an exercise in just staying still, no progress to be made. She felt sure that she would topple backwards and fear spiked through her at the vision of herself lying helpless on the pavement, trampled by each leather-shod foot, unable to rise because the weight of her bag kept her pinned to the ground.

Wriggling through the faceless city-bound mass, she made her way to the edge of the bridge and gripped the railing tightly. She stood looking out across the river, watching the wind play across the surface of the water until the rush of the crowd had dissipated. She felt a buzz on her wrist. Her watch was telling her that she was late for work. She laughed at how easy it was to pull it from her wrist and toss it into the river.

A bubble of levity worked its way up from her chest, and she ripped open the bag at her feet and began to pull items from it and hurl them into the river. The lycra leggings she wore to the gym, designed to make her bum look fuller, but not too full. The aluminium water bottle to ensure she stayed hydrated. The self-help book that told her how to lean-in, be a girl-boss, be authentic, stop caring, be more caring, only work four hours a week but always be working. The laptop she carried to and from the office each day because there was no such thing as 'off'. The pretty pastel-coloured individually wrapped tampons that looked like lollies as they fluttered out across the water.

She could feel the eyes of the passing pedestrians on her. One woman grabbed the hand of the small boy she was with and pulled him closer, away from the 'crazy lady'. She didn't care. It was freeing, cathartic, this offering she made to the river. *Take it all*, she thought, *Take it and keep it, I never want it back.*

With a final shout of joy, she hurled the now empty bag over the side of the bridge. The wind caught it and it filled up momentarily like a leather balloon until gravity won out and the bag, too, met the surface of the water where it was pulled downstream. She watched until the bag passed under the next bridge and began to sink out of sight, the river carrying away her offerings and, with them, the identity of the woman she had tried so hard to be.

Unsure of her direction, she began to walk, abandoning her usual, purposeful stride and drifting slowly through the crowded streets, taking paths she had never trod, until she reached the park, an oasis of stillness ringed by tall glass towers. The trees glowed copper and gold in the sunlight and she lay back on the grass and gazed up at the colourful canopy.

A sharp pain at her sternum drew her out of her reverie and she sat up, feeling the wire of her bra digging into her skin. Glancing around to be sure she was alone, she quickly pulled her shirt over her head, and then reached behind herself to undo the clasp. The relief was immediate as the pressure abated and she quickly extricated herself from the web of fastenings and wires. As she did so, she could see the livid red marks on her skin that the wire had made. Pulling the shirt back on, she balled up the peach lace and launched it skyward

where it caught in the branches of the trees, straps fluttering and twisting like a strange bird.

She got up and kept walking. The wind whipped her hair up around her face and she was surprised to see a small yellow leaf, still stuck there from when she had left her home hours ago. Her steps were lighter, her breath easier as she wound her way through the paths and lawns of the park. She took off her trainers to feel the soft grass beneath her feet and left them behind, by the side of a small pond where she had stopped to dip her feet into the cool, moss-green water. It occurred to her that for the first time she could recall, no one knew where she was. Not her parents, not her husband or colleagues or friends. No one could reach her or track her. She was entirely alone.

\*\*\*

The sun began to descend behind the city and unconsciously she found herself turning her steps back toward the river, toward home. The pavements became busier the deeper into the city she got, and she felt the weight of more than one gaze on her unconfined breasts and her bare feet. Her headphones were long discarded and the sounds of the street, dagger-like, pierced the shield of tranquillity she had wrapped around herself over the course of the day. She folded her arms across her chest, hunching in on herself, trying to make herself less conspicuous. Her steps became slower as she felt the weight of the stares drag against her skin. A man stopped her, concern in his eyes, a gentle hand on her arm, "You alright, love?"

She looked down at where his fingers rested on the fabric of her sleeve, the touch felt alien, intrusive, and she snatched away her arm.

"Calm down, I'm just tryna help you." The man looked injured as she brushed past him and continued on. "Fuckin bitch," he muttered. The curse wasn't meant for her hearing, but the wind carried it to her anyway, and she felt guilty for her ingratitude, and then indignant at her guilt. She walked on, past the brightly lit office buildings, the yellow stone churches, the school where a row of children, paired two-by-two, laughingly boarded a bus.

Her earlier lightness was draining away. The river had only granted her a temporary reprieve when it washed away her offerings. With each step, she felt the ties that bound her re-establishing themselves. The expectations of her husband, of their families, of the strangers she passed in the street, weighed down upon her, asking her to contort, conform, concede. She reached the river, but rather than cross the bridge toward the station, she descended the narrow stone steps and stood on the pebbly bank that was uncovered when the river was at its lowest ebb.

Her skin felt hot and tight, despite the autumn wind which blew cooler now that the sun was sinking. She pulled off her top and kicked off her trousers, pulling down with them the scrap of peach lace, its partner abandoned hours earlier to adorn the trees in the park. The lingerie had been a gift from *her* mother, who believed less in old wives' tales and more in the fifty ways to spice up your bedroom tips from her glossy magazines. Looking down she saw that the peach lace was now stained rust-brown with blood, and she felt a hot spike of bitter satisfaction.

She stood naked, in the shadow of the bridge, unseen by the suited army as it began its weary march homeward. A wave of cramps rippled across her abdomen and she pressed her hands into her body, pushing against the place from where the pain radiated. Here was another kind of heaviness. Heavy was the weight of the unshed blood. Heavy too, the weight of hope. The hopes of her parents and their desire for a legacy. The dreams of his parents, their yearning to pass on their name, their family stories, their nose. The intense pressure of her husband's search for life's meaning, all of it centred on this small, empty hollow inside her body.

*It's too much,* she thought, *it's too heavy. I can't carry this.*

Sinking to her knees, she began to crawl along the stony bank, casting out her hands until she found what she was looking for, sharp-edged and cold. It was a piece of flint, one edge worn to a fine blade. She waded out deeper into the river until it lapped at her thighs. The water was cold in the shadow of the bridge, but she welcomed the numbness that it brought her. She had thought that morning that she had given everything she had to the river, offerings to be washed away so that she could be reborn. She realised now that she had given the river only the superficial trappings, the easy sacrifices. It wasn't enough, she had not given up herself.

With one hand, she firmly cupped her breast, and with the other, she drew the stony blade across her skin until a line of blood welled up. Again and again, she cut, through skin, then fat, then glands, until finally she pulled her breast away from her body and held it in her hand. Gently, she bent down and let it slip into the water. Then she stood, and taking her other breast in hand, repeated the process, quicker this time, more confident in her cuts. She wondered why she didn't feel more pain. Perhaps she was too numb from the wind and water that chilled her skin.

As she began to cut into her abdomen, her legs gave way. *It's shock,* she thought, *that's why there's no pain.*

She let herself fall backward until she was floating on the water, and the river carried her out from under the shadow of the bridge and into the patch of water that the sun was painting gold with its last efforts of the day. She thought she heard a scream from the bridge, but the water covered her ears, and the world was blissfully muted once more. She worked now by touch alone, opening her belly and feeling inside until she pulled out the soft empty pouch that was the focus of so much of her family's consternation. She tugged a little harder and felt it tear softly from her body, trailing fleshy tubes and ovaries as it too was released into the water.

The shouts became louder and she could see people running on the banks. They didn't understand. She was lighter now. Free. The golden water poured in and filled the holes she had carved in her body, washing away the blood and smoothing the jagged edges, knitting them back together, making her anew. She could feel the river's acceptance of her sacrifice, washing away the curse of her birth, of her sex, washing away the lingering traces of every unwelcome gaze and unwanted touch, every judgement and expectation. The soft, lapping waters carried her gently back to the river's edge until she felt the silt of the shore beneath her hands and she pushed herself upright. She stood there,

on the bank and she felt as light as one of the autumn leaves tangled in her hair. She opened her mouth and laughter poured out, rich and deep and joyous.

A crowd was growing on the embankment and she saw a man in uniform approaching her with a bright silver blanket. He wrapped it around her shoulders, his face drawn tight with concern.

"What happened? I heard someone had fallen in. Are you ok?"

She opened her mouth to tell him that she was fine, but only laughter came and so she spread her arms wide, the silver blanket unfurling behind her like foil wings, to show him the gift that the river had given her.

But she had not understood what it meant to be free of burdens, had not realised it was they that kept her tethered to the ground, and now she was so light, too light. The wind caught her up, silver wings and leaves and laughter, and carried her into the darkening sky. She heard the shouts of the people on the ground, but they became smaller and smaller until all she could hear was the sound of her own laughter, echoing back to her on the wind.

There was nothing left to carry.

# DRONES AND DOMINIONS

## BY MATTHEW R. DAVIS

All children dream of flying, and Adele was no exception. As a little girl, she'd soared through sunny skies on wings of gossamer; as a teenager, she'd navigated stormier climes with dun-coloured feathers that shone silver under moonlight; and always, she'd looked up at passing planes with the surety that one day she, too, would ride the tides of the air. And now, at forty-seven, she often followed her job to three cities in a single month, and each time she took flight, she also took comfort in the thought that certainty could, in time, become fact. It was simply a matter of belief.

But tonight, she boarded the plane to Hobart wearing a dread so heavy she could have checked it at the luggage counter. Departure had been pushed back two hours, and her ears rang with a doleful resonance. She could almost feel a hot, hungry breath on the nape of her neck.

Adele twitched a smile at the welcoming flight attendant and edged down the aisle, coffee clutched in one hand like a protective talisman. It wasn't just the caffeine that had her pulse bolting like a spooked horse, nor the airport bar vodkas she'd employed the coffee to counter. *Two hours,* she thought, remembering the restless impotence she'd felt waiting for the delayed flight—squirming in her seat, her eyes skimming over and over the same paragraph of a Colleen Hoover paperback. *How far can a dream travel in two hours?*

Her seat was 13, in Row M. Two thirteens, back-to-back. She told herself she didn't believe in luck, then wondered why else someone would climb repeatedly into metal tubes that were thrown through thin air miles above the jealous earth. Faith in technology? Sure, but a little old-fashioned good fortune would be desperately welcomed right now.

Adele took her seat by the window, carry-on in her lap, and waited to be hemmed in. Soon the agent of her captivity appeared, broad enough to spill over the armrest into Adele's personal space and talking even before she'd buckled herself in. Adele slipped on her professional smile, recognising the irony—once it had been she who'd treated her fellow passengers as a captive audience, and now, when she wanted only to be left alone, her past indulgences were coming back to haunt her.

"What about you, then?" Andrea had been visiting her sister in Sydney, had two kids in primary school, a husband fixated on protein shakes now he'd quit smoking—all this before Adele had managed to give her own name. "Heading home?"

"No," Adele said. She hadn't seen her Parramatta apartment for almost a week, nor a bed of any kind. "I just need to get away for a while."

"Tasmania's good for that, all right. What do you do?"

"I'm a FIFO HR consultant."

"Uh-oh, someone flies around terminating people," Andrea quipped, and Adele couldn't hide a twitch of unease at her phrasing. "Sorry! Bad joke. Born with both feet in my mouth, me."

"That's fine. Don't mind me, I'm just *really* tired."

Andrea opened her mouth, closed it, and Adele knew what she'd thought better of saying: *you look it.* "Not sleeping well?"

"No." Adele had been snatching a couple of hours a day on terminal benches and airplane seats; she hadn't lain down in so long that it felt like a unique kind of self-torture. "I'm going to try tonight, though, so don't think I'm rude if I…"

"Not at all!" Andrea bubbled. "You go right ahead."

Adele opened her carry-on. Most of its contents were clothes in need of washing, but that luxury was currently beyond her, so she simply bought tourist T-shirts and fresh underwear as needed—she was currently clad in a duty-free tee emblazoned with a cartoon frog cake and the word RADELAIDE, a steep step down from her usual business attire. She found what she was looking for and unwound the cord.

What Adele liked best about planes these days was the constant noise, the chatter of passengers overriding her own thoughts, the dull roar of engines drowning out any other drones in her head. But every so often she needed to block all that out and face the truth, and noise-cancelling headphones did the trick. She slipped the speakers over her ears, reducing the surrounding hubbub to a whisper at the edges of her hearing. Now she was left with the throb of her own heartbeat, comfortingly loud…and louder still, the ringing-cymbal drone she'd been fleeing for a week.

*So close! Come on, let's get this fucking crate in the air!*

Adele slipped off the headphones, composed a neutral expression, took a swig of coffee. That was what ordinary people did. Ordinary people wouldn't still hear the resonance of that drone beneath everything else, wouldn't have been hearing its unchanging pitch swell and fade for days on end, wouldn't carry that tone with them into dreams that made true rest an impossibility.

Flight attendants now hit their marks in the aisles, career dancers ready to perform their signature routine for the thousandth time. The closest was a white woman with hay-blonde hair scraped into a perfect bun, her face the spotless mask of a Maybelline model; the other was a beautiful Asian man, not a single dark hair or uniform crease out of place. Adele admired the dedication required to achieve this kind of elegance—she'd gotten her bathroom mirror prep down to fifteen minutes and resented even that, eager to get on with her day—but tonight, these exemplars of beauty only made her feel bedraggled and haggard by comparison. She'd been washing at airport bathroom basins, had done little more lately than apply deodorant and some basic eyeliner to soften the bags beneath.

The attendants carried on with their choreography, moving in time to the pre-recorded announcement—slipping on deflated life vests, pointing to emergency lights on their shoulders, brandishing plastic whistles attached by nylon cords. Adele lost interest in the charade and retrieved her paperback. She wouldn't actually read it—books had failed her this week, her brain unable to fix on the flow of the prose—but it gave her a shield against Andrea's curiosity, made her look like a regular passenger having a regular flight. Not a desperate woman clinging to shreds of ritual, so tired the world around her felt warm and taffy-soft, driven almost to madness by the constant drone only she could hear.

It had all started with the man in the bar. God, but didn't it always? There had been many men in many bars in many cities, and some of those encounters had turned sour enough to leave Adele wishing she'd never even made eye contact—but she regretted none as ardently as this.

The bar was in the Novotel hotel at Brisbane Airport, and his name was Burton. They were both flying out in the morning, returning home from a successful mission, and he was fiftyish, rugged, well-dressed—perfect pre-flight entertainment. His gaze had a haunted cast to it like he was trying to forget something, and he fucked that way, too, head down and eyes squeezed shut. He got the job done well enough, though, and Adele preferred detached vigour to a cloying, clingy, I'll-always-remember-you intimacy. Even better, Burton fell asleep almost as soon as she rolled herself and the condom off him, removing the burden of small talk.

That part of the encounter went as smoothly as she could've hoped. It was what happened when she tried to leave his hotel suite that changed everything.

Returning from Burton's bathroom,

Adele had set about gathering her clothes. She'd discarded them with a single-minded abandon—stockings draped over the bedside lamp, pencil skirt shoved under the pillow, bra tossed across the room to land on a table. She'd crossed over to pick up this last item, and when she did, her fingers caught and dragged away the cloth it had fallen upon.

The object it had been covering was a carved wooden arch perhaps eighteen inches tall, with a burnished bronze disc suspended from chains within. A small gong, then, and quite old, judging by the wear on its dark oaken bones and the hypnotic rococo patterns carved into them; it had seemed to watch when Adele stepped back to slip into her bra, a hungry eye with an empty plate for a pupil. A bone-handled striker hung on one side, its head a perfect sphere that may have been a black pearl.

An unusual thing to find in a hotel room most nights, but Burton had grunted "antiquities" when she'd asked after his line of work. The tabletop around it was littered with papers, so he must have been doing research before heading down to the bar for a few cognacs and an unforeseen assignation with a human resources consultant. Adele could understand his interest – the gong was intriguing, with no cultural markers she could readily identify, and it must have been worth a pretty penny to justify Burton's expedition. She'd carefully grasped the striker between two fingers and lifted it closer to the bedside lamp to see if the head was, indeed, a genuine black pearl.

"What are you doing?"

Adele flinched and shot upright, dropping the striker. Its head had struck the bronze disc, and a low, sonorous tone rung out loud enough to be heard in the next room. Burton was awake, staring like he'd caught her trying to leg it out of his suite with the antique clutched to her chest.

"Sorry, I was just…it looked like…sorry."

This naked stranger, who'd been inside her mere minutes before, had turned his shocked gaze to the shimmering bronze. The note she'd sounded was still ringing, lingering like white noise from an untuned radio. He'd looked desperate to leap off the bed and pinch the gong into silence, but his tensed muscles didn't move him an inch.

"Do you have any idea what you've just done?"

"It was an accident!" she protested. "You startled me."

Burton had closed his eyes, shaking his head like a father learning his child has committed an unconscionable crime.

"Look, I'm *sorry*. I'm going now, anyway—"

"Do you know what that is?" he'd asked.

"I—well… it looks like a dinner gong."

Burton's eyes opened, glistening in the low light. "*Exactly.*"

Adele had had enough. She fetched her blouse, scooped up her stockings and heels, found her handbag on the floor.

"Okay, I'm off. Safe travels, Burton."

She was at the door, back turned to obscure her rueful expression, when he'd asked, "Can you still hear it?"

"I can." The sustain of the accidental strike had still been humming at the edge of her hearing. "How long does a gong go on, anyway?"

"It's when it stops that you'll need to worry."

She hadn't known how to reply to that, so she opened the door instead. She'd turned to nod farewell as it closed behind her, and the last she saw of Burton, he'd been staring at the gong as though it were a bomb that had begun to tick.

Adele returned to her room, showered, changed into her sleeping clothes. She'd slipped into bed, enjoying the warm throb of her used body, and set her phone alarm before killing the light. Strangely, she'd found the sound of the gong still ringing inside her head.

It was so persistent it even crossed over, unbroken, into her dreams.

As when a girl, she'd found herself flying through the night, cruising low and silent along darkened streets she didn't recognise. The air around her streaked and pulsed with an intricate and ever-changing rainbow web of lights that she instinctively understood to be the invisible nervous system of the modern world—wi-fi signals, radio and TV transmissions, telephone connections—and the bones of buildings were lit up like neon skeletons by coursing electricity. The hum of the gong's sustain was constant, her flight so smooth she had no sense of a body's encumbrance. She might have been an airborne camera on remote control, a drone within a drone.

When she'd woken the next morning, she'd barely felt rested at all—and the lingering chime of the gong was, if anything, a couple of decibels louder.

*If only you hadn't touched that fucking thing, Dell, then maybe—*

Someone touched her, and she jerked away, snatching off the headphones.

"Sorry! Here we go," Andrea announced, and the plane commenced taxiing along the runway. Adele focused on the building roar of engines, trying to drown the ever-present drone in industrial noise. Then she was pressed back into her seat as the jet's nose edged into the air, taking flight once more.

*Tell me it was soon enough.* The gong's hum hadn't appreciably softened, but it must. *Tell me I'll be safe across the water, at least for a day or two.*

The only way to be sure: deny the caffeine's charge and let her dreams provide the answer.

It was the dreams that had convinced her something weird was afoot. The constant low-level presence of the gong strike was strange, yes, but that could be chalked up to short-term tinnitus caused by sudden noise in a quiet room. The *dreams,* though—always the same, and yet not. In her own bed the night after returning to Sydney, she'd found herself cruising low over churning black waves—crossing a sea, perhaps, as that surreal aurora of digital signals seethed in the air around her. The journey had seemed to last all night, and just before waking, she'd seen a coastline heaving into view.

Adele had returned to the office, occasionally shaking her head to dislodge the perpetual ringing. It had nagged at her all day, distracting her from conversation with her colleagues, and more than one remarked that she looked tired. She'd claimed to be coming down with something and, after a rapid antigen test showed negative, accepted the suggestion of some time off. She had plenty of leave accrued since her life revolved around work and travel, her socialising largely comprised of drinks with strangers in hotel bars, so that wasn't a problem.

The ringing, however, continued to be.

And when Adele crashed into bed that night, her breath sour with red wine, she'd dreamed she was soaring over streets she knew—Paramatta streets, only a few minutes' drive from her apartment. The air was laced with those ever-shifting rainbow clouds of digital noise, glowing maps of human communications pinging spaceward to satellites and back, but no bluster of traffic, no café or car stereo, no birdsong blemished the unbroken swell of the gong's drone. As she'd drawn ever nearer to her own street, she'd passed an electronic billboard she saw every morning and night when she was in town. The date it displayed was current, the time accurate to the second.

All at once, Adele had understood the truth of the matter.

She wasn't flying at all. This wasn't even her dream.

This was *live.*

She had been seeing through eyes that were not her own, and they were following her, and they were *so close.*

Adele had thrashed awake as if splashed with water, the drone so loud she could barely hear her own heartbeat. Her flight response kicked in hard, and she didn't question it. A woman learned to trust her gut, and hers was screaming at her to *run.*

Adele hadn't yet unpacked her rolling case since returning from her Brisbane trip, and she'd blessed that oversight as she grabbed keys and phone and hauled it all from her apartment like the place was on fire. She tore out of the parking lot, saw nothing unusual in the sky—no nightmare swooping down the city's byways toward her. But the drone was growing loud enough to feel in her bones, so she'd driven blindly on into the night. It was ten minutes before she'd realised instinct was taking her along a route she followed almost every week. She was heading for the airport.

She pulled up in the terminal parking garage and changed in the front seat, wriggling into creased clothes from her Brisbane assignment. The drone had dulled a touch, assuring her she'd put some distance between herself and whatever was coming, and she'd known what she had to do. Heading inside the terminal, she'd booked herself on the next available flight out, a redeye to Canberra. And then she'd dragged her flight case to the deserted gate, bought a strong coffee, and awaited her deliverance.

That was the last night she'd slept in a bed, the last night she'd felt even remotely safe. Since then, she'd racked up thousands of kilometres in the air—from Canberra to Adelaide, Adelaide to Perth, Perth to Darwin, Darwin to Sydney, always moving. She snatched a few hours of sleep sitting at airport gates, in passenger seats thousands of feet above the earth, and each time she returned to the vision: flying silently through data-streaked skies, across benighted desert plains, along signal-stained city streets. The drone rang on and on, and whatever rode it was equally ceaseless, never pausing for rest nor giving any clue as to its true nature. She woke each time to a tone in her head that grew softer or louder every hour, a constant warning no-one else could hear.

She had roused something when she struck that gong, and the summoning would not go unanswered—that, or her sanity was glitching hard. But Adele was a woman who knew and trusted her own mind, and to give over to such doubts

now would be treason. She'd lasted forty-seven years by believing in her instincts, and even if they sometimes led her into regrettable encounters, she always walked away unharmed. She'd turned down a tipsy car ride that had ended in a fatal crash, spurned a man she later learned had been arrested for assaulting partners, refused to lease an apartment soon revealed to be infested with cockroaches. Her gut spoke truth, and she listened.

A week after that first desperate flight, she was still ahead of the dream, ahead of the drone. She was bone-weary and her skin felt like week-old foundation and she longed for a hot shower, a soft bed, a single minute's true silence…but still she ran. Were there any other recourse, she'd take it—but she had no idea how to find and contact Burton, and internet searches had drawn a blank on anything even remotely like this. Help from other quarters was not forthcoming.

And so she flew.

The plane levelled off now, and Adele glanced out the window to see a ruffled bed of cloud in the night sky below; it might have been a lunar landscape, had it not been lit by the moon itself. She put on the headphones, listened to the drone. Was it quieter? It must have faded by some small degree, but it was hard to tell. Still, once she'd put the Bass Strait and a few hundred kilometres between herself and the mainland, she'd know if she'd bought herself a little more of a lead on her fate.

"Dinner is served!"

Andrea, no great respecter of boundaries, touched her arm again—the immaculate attendants were pushing a service cart along the aisle, offering coffee and biscuits. Adele's stomach growled, but she shook her throbbing skull and laid it back against the headrest, closing her eyes. She'd be fine, she just needed to escape on the inside as well as the outside for a minute. She was going to be okay. After all, she was flying.

She felt herself rushing through the darkness at almost a thousand kilometres per hour, and then she opened eyes that weren't hers and the hunger was still there, pulsing like the points of light in the night ahead. Racing toward them arrow-fast, a hawk swooping upon a heedless sparrow.

Impact with no sound or impedance. Swallowed up into a dark, hollow space, and then spat back out into the light. A narrow corridor pulsing with electric nerves. The interior of a commercial passenger plane.

*This* plane.

Hovering unseen down the aisle, passing over the service cart, unnoticed by smiling attendants and chatting commuters. Slowing at the midsection, turning to the right.

Seeing Andrea in profile, ignorant of scrutiny—and beyond her, an exhausted woman sleeping with headphones clamped to her ears.

Edging forward across the aisle seat—reaching out—

Adele opened her eyes with a startled cry. Andrea jerked back, her extended hand hovering uncertainly in the air.

"Whoa! Are you all right, Dell?"

"I…what…wait, did you—"

"You looked like you were having a nightmare."

Adele wrestled her heaving lungs into a semblance of calm. The flight attendants were standing in the aisle behind Andrea, observing with expressions of professional concern.

"Would you like some water?" the blonde asked.

"No!"

"Here," her elegant colleague said, passing her a glass anyway, and Andrea's meddling hand knocked it. Water splashed into Adele's face, and she spluttered. It was cold, brackish.

"No!" she cried again. The denial rang out clear and untrammelled, drawing her notice to something that should have been immediately apparent.

The quiet.

She could hear faint shrieking, someone watching a horror movie on their phone perhaps, but all underlying noise had ceased.

"The drone!" Adele cried. "It's gone! Oh, Christ—it's *over!*"

Relief flooded her like a physical substance, and she coughed so hard she might've been choking up all those days of stress. Andrea watched her, downcast, as if about to bear sad tidings. The blonde attendant leaned forward with a pen torch and flashed it a couple of times, perhaps testing Adele's faculties. Her colleague was pouring another glass of water.

"No more of that, please! What's going on? Why are you looking at me like that?"

Silence for a moment, complete other than the distant chorus of shrill whistles from the inconsiderate passenger's phone video.

"Do you remember what Burton said?" Andrea asked.

"What? How could you know—" Adele spluttered again as the male attendant leaned forward to offer her the glass, clumsily spilling the water over her mouth. "Fucking hell! Will you stop that! What do you mean about Burton? He just asked me…"

*Can you still hear it?*

But why would that matter, unless—

*It's when it stops that you'll need to worry.*

Adele froze as she wiped water from her parched lips, beginning to understand. She stared at Andrea, the attendants, the passengers. They all stared back with pearl-black eyes, still and silent as statues.

"I haven't woken up, have I?"

Andrea shook her head. "But at least this is your own dream now. The drone has stopped, and so have the visions. This is all you."

"But… isn't that *good?*"

"Depends. You could be awake if you want… but it seems you don't. So, the question is: what could be so bad you'd rather sleep through it?"

"Tell me."

"Are you sure you want to know?"

"Yes." Whilst certainty had been ever-present of late—she must *run*—knowledge had not, and Adele needed its ballast. "Say it!"

Andrea and the attendants watched her, waiting, poised like mannequins. Adele's gut was going haywire, on high alert and unable to ascertain why—until she realised why the silence was so complete.

The hum of the gong was not the only thing that had ended. There was another drone she could no longer hear, and this one's absence was chilling.

The plane's engines had stopped.

Andrea nodded sadly as Adele gripped her armrests in terror. "Here we go, then. The terrible truth. Ding dong, Dell."

The male attendant leaned close and dashed another glass of water in Adele's face, and she gasped and spluttered, and

when she opened her eyes, the lights of the plane were gone. The sky was wide open above her and black as could be, and she was *freezing*, and when a cold, salty crest broke across her face, she realised it was a wave.

She was bobbing in the deep dark sea, kept afloat by an inflated life vest that someone had put on her. Adele screamed, was silenced by a wet slap of brine, choked in panic. Her vision was flickering— no, that was the small emergency light attached to the shoulder of her vest. She flailed in the water, managing to turn herself a few degrees to the left, and saw the enormous tail of her ditched plane sinking into the sea some fifty metres away, lights dying as the fuselage slipped deeper into the wet mouth of the world. In a few seconds, the passenger jet would be swallowed whole.

*This is another dream! WAKE UP!*

But no dream could ever feel so intense as this. The cold cut right through her, and her heart sank faster than the drowning plane.

*"HELP!"* she screamed. *"HELP ME!"*

She realised now that she could hear other desperate cries, distant as if played on a phone by an inconsiderate passenger, and the high-pitched wails of blown whistles. Recalling the emergency procedures she'd sat through so many times, she fumbled until she found the nylon cord and reeled in the plastic mouthpiece, brought it up to salt-parched lips and blew.

The whistle was piercingly loud, and Adele realised how far away her fellow survivors must be. Somehow, she'd been separated from them after they'd carried her dreaming body off the crashed plane.

But she could still see them, their shoulder lights glowing on the water's surface like floating fireflies.

She'd spent long days avoiding other people because she had no way of telling them what she was experiencing. But now, in this darkest hour, she needed their company more than anything. Calling on faded memories of swimming lessons, Adele began to paddle toward the nearest cluster of beacons.

She'd barely moved before she noticed the frantic cries and whistles were thinning out, as though survivors were weakening in the chilly water. But that wasn't all. As she watched across the shifting surface of the sea, their shoulder-mounted lights began to blink out, one by one.

*"HEY!"*

What could this be? Hypothermic drowning? *Sharks?* Adele froze, suddenly sure that something dire was cutting ever closer, homing in on her position.

The whistles fell silent, and a few final ragged screams rang out over the terrible tides. Adele could see only a scant number of scattered lights now, bobbing on the undulating surface, and each time she blinked away a faceful of bitter water, she counted less.

Until finally she could see no lights, hear no screams.

Only the ceaseless drone of the waves.

She was alone.

Her gut did not agree. Raw instinct insisted that she was observed, approached, *known.* And though she could see nothing in any direction now other than the waves, not even the empennage of the downed plane, Adele could feel something rising inside her, a swelling of volume. This drone was not audible, but it resonated in every bone of her body, every cell of her soul, as though she herself were a gong struck to summon unknowable appetites. She flapped her arms, desperate to take flight one last time, but all dreams were done.

The vibration reached an unbearable intensity that threatened to shake her to pieces, reaching its peak when perception's veil parted and Adele, seasoned by sea salt, laid terrified eyes on her ravening pursuer at last.

Dinner was served.

# WINNER OF THE AUSTRALIAN SHADOWS AWARD FOR BEST EDITED WORK 2020

ISSUE 15

# MIDNIGHT ECHO

EDITED BY
LEE MURRAY

Featuring
JOANNE ANDERTON
JAY CASELBERG
TOM DULLEMOND
JASON FRANKS
REBECCA FRASER
ANTHONY PAUL FERGUSON
J.A. HAIGH
MELANIE HARDING-SHAW
JULEIGH HOWARD-HOBSON
NIKKY LEE
MARTIN LIVINGS
STUART OLVER
DAVID SCHEMBRI
DEBORAH SHELDON
ALISSA SMITH

The Magazine of the Australasian Horror Writers A...

AHWA

# ARISAN

## BY FEBY IDRUS

Opa had grey eyes. Beautiful, yes; striking, of course; but, at the end of the day, just another sign of contamination. Courtesy of the Europeans who colonised our Indonesian islands so long ago that their whiteness has become a part of us, whether we like it or not. I mean, I call my grandfather Opa, for goodness' sake. A Dutch word. And now that we all live here, in a former English colony, sunk deep in English language, I'm not even sure I still remember the Bahasa word for Opa. I look at Opa's eyes, and my mother's nearly white skin, and my too-tall frame, and our sharp teeth, and I think: our blood has been dirtied. Made impure.

My mother said to me once, "Sita. It happen so long ago. Why still so mad all the time? It's like a disease with you. Just enjoy life, ok? Just relax. Eat something." As we all know, every ill can be fixed by eating something. That's the Indonesian way; we're eaters. We've even got a word for getting together with your whole extended family and having a meal that starts at lunchtime and keeps going until the evening and it happens every month at a different family member's house and it's for getting together and being together and eating as a family. White folks don't really have one word for this. But our one word is arisan.

So it was kind of a big deal to invite Luke to this month's arisan. I think he thought this was going to be a normal 'meet the parents' thing, until I explained to him on the way over what arisan actually was. "Wait. Your *entire* family?" he asked.

"Yeah. My cousins want to meet you. My aunts. My aunt who isn't really an aunt, she's my dad's second cousin but we call her an aunt anyway. All of them."

"How many people are gonna be there?"

"Dunno. Depends who decides to turn up."

"Oh, so it might not be that many."

"Yeah. Maybe only thirty or forty."

"*What?*"

"Oh calm down."

"Thirty or forty of your relatives? How do you even have so many?"

"How do you have so few?"

Luke paused his panic for a moment. His lips pursed. "Am I going to be the only white person there?"

"Probably. Now you'll know how it feels."

Luke sighed. "Do you have to do that?"

"Do what?"

"You know." He waved his hands around indeterminately. "Make it about race stuff."

My hands tensed around the steering wheel. "May I remind *you* that you were the one who brought up race by asking if you'd be the only white person there—"

"You didn't have to say, *Now you'll know how it—*"

"But now you will know how it feels to be outnumbered. That's normal life for me. Finally, you're entering my world. You'd think you'd recognise the opportunity for growth. Jesus Christ."

"You shouldn't take the Lord's name in vain."

I'm going to kill him. "My people are Muslim," I said as we finally turned into my parents' driveway. "Christian shit doesn't apply to us."

Pairs of shoes, at least fifteen of them, lay scattered by the front door. I slipped off mine and knocked on the ajar door while Luke struggled to pry off his hightop Converses. "Assalamulaikum!" I called out. Myriad voices inside called back, "Walaikumsalam!"

My mother came toward me, arms out for an embrace. Her expression was taut. When she hugged me, she hissed close to my ear, "Can you talk to your Opa please? He refuses to eat."

I jerked back to look at her more closely. "How long has this been going on?"

"A month. He only eats a tiny tiny bit. He's so difficult! It makes me want to scream." She looked over my shoulder and perked up, moving me out of the way (because a nubile young man is way more interesting than your own daughter). "Come, come!" she exclaimed to Luke, reverting to English. "I'm Sita's mother. Come in!"

Luke gingerly stepped over the threshold, his uncertainty clearly battling his need to be polite. "I'm Luke, nice to meet you," he said. He had a hole in his right sock. His big toe stuck out, crassly.

Each person he was introduced to oohed and aahed and sized him up as if they'd never seen a white guy in real life before.

I left Luke in the front room, swamped by cousins and aunts and uncles, and went into the dining room. There, beside a long table laid with a white tablecloth and dotted with woven rattan placemats, my Opa sat, hunched, in an aged wooden chair. I knelt beside him. "Opa," I said, looking closely up into his eyes. "How are you?"

Opa's eyes seemed not just grey but clouded. "Tired," he muttered in answer.

"You need to eat, Opa."

His head bobbed like a palm frond. The bones of his shoulders pushed up like shards of mountain peak under his light brown jersey. His face had lost its cheeks, and his fingers were a strange dark bluish colour that showed through despite his light brown skin. I took his thin hand. With effort, he looked at me. His grey eyes held me there. *I want to die.* His words were faint, barely discernible. *I'm tired of living.*

I heard my heartbeat throb hard in my temples. "Don't say that," I hissed. "I don't want you to die. How dare you? How *dare* you. You gave all of us life and now you just want to give up on your own?"

Opa's lips curved, a mild crescent moon. He tapped my hand, and I realised how tight I had been squeezing his. *So angry,* he chided. *Aren't you tired of being always so angry?*

"What are you talking about? You're the one who taught me it's good to be angry. It gives you power."

Opa huffed out a dry laugh. "Power?" he said out loud. "You know how many powerful people I see die? All of them— weak. We are all weak in the end." He released my hand, and I understood that I was dismissed.

When I found Luke again, he was on the settee in the front room, propped up by silk-covered pouffes embroidered by one of my cousins. The intricately carved teak coffee table was dotted with glass jars, cut-glass bowls and plates of pastries and cakes. All the glass jars had their lids off. Luke held a white saucer piled with tiny pastries and cakes, and a glass of orange cordial sat on the intricately carved teak coffee table in front of him, no doubt brought for Luke by my youngest female cousin. "These are really good," Luke mumbled through a mouthful of putri salju. I could smell the sucrose on his breath from the doorway.

"Yes, I know. You're aware we're eating a full meal soon, right? You eat all that, you won't be able to manage a meal."

"Oh Sita," Tante Minda scolded as she passed. "Your boyfriend so skinny."

"We just trying to fatten him up, ok?" Tante Venita chimed in.

"Make him nice and healthy," Tante An added. She winked at me.

"Yeah, Sita," Luke said, reaching for a piece of kue lapis. When he popped it in his mouth, his brow furrowed. "This reminds me of something."

"Spekkoek?"

"Yes! That's it! My gran's best friend Anneke used to make it."

"Yeah. This kind of kue lapis is basically the same."

"Oh, so Indonesians stole it from the Dutch?"

Screw you, I thought. "Considering the recipe requires nutmeg, and nutmeg comes from Indonesia, *actually*, the Dutch took it from us."

Luke rolled his eyes. I wanted to strangle him. Instead, I buttoned my lips together,

sat down, and picked up a piece of kue lapis. I studied its thin alternating layers: chocolate brown, pale gold, chocolate brown again. *Aren't you tired of being so angry?* Opa had asked me. I couldn't even understand the question. Anger protects you. Anger is an adrenaline shot in the arm. It shocks you to act. Anger is a cattle prod. A whip.

"Ayo!" Tante Rita called, clapping her hands. "Makan!"

"What does that mean?" Luke whispered.

"'Come on, let's eat,'" I translated. I nudged his knee. "Go." My mother flapped her hand at him, further encouraging him.

Luke half-stood up, then noticed I stayed sitting. "Aren't you eating?"

"The men eat first," I answered.

"What?" Luke glanced around. Several uncles were already lined up at the now-laden tables, filling their plates with nasi kuning and dendeng belado. The women were still passing in and out of the kitchen, fetching flat white rice spoons and extra placemats, still working while the men served themselves.

"The men eat first," I repeated. "Then the kids. Then the women. Women eat last."

"Are you serious?"

"Yes."

"But that's *wrong!*" Luke said, too loudly. "That's so *backward!*" My mother glanced over, her gaze at Luke noticeably cooler than when she invited him in.

"Stop it," I said. "This is how we do it. Don't call my people backward."

"It's misogynistic."

"It's how it is."

"I'm not participating in this."

"Excuse me, how many female priests are there at your church? Yeah. Exactly. Don't get sniffy at me about misogyny. Go fill your goddamn plate."

Luke shoved himself off the settee. When he was safely lined up at the serving table, Oom Arno explaining the food to him, I went to my mother, who still looked a little chilly. "Are you ready to eat?" I asked her.

"Yes," my mother answered without hesitating.

Luke gingerly balanced a couple of pieces of kerupuk on the edge of his plate, otherwise piled high with nasi kuning, pergedel, dendeng belado and fresh vegetables. Just beyond him, Opa sat, still hunched. The plate in front of him held a spoonful of yellow rice and a wizened piece of fried chicken. "Do you think Opa will eat?" I asked.

My mother considered. "Maybe. I hope so." She flapped her hand at me. "Go on."

When I returned from the kitchen, Luke still stood in front of Opa, talking and stuffing his face at the same time. Opa had not touched his food. Luke looked up as I approached. "Oh hey, I've been looking for you. What's with the knife?"

I took Luke's laden plate, placed it neatly on the table beside him with my left hand, then raised my right hand and with the chef's knife I'd gotten from the kitchen I slashed Luke across the chest. Not deeply; just enough for a pencil line of red to slowly appear across Luke's white shirt. He stared up at me, his mouth open.

The smell of his blood in the air quietened the room. Everyone watched us now. Tante Rita, Tante An, Tante Venita, Tante Minda, my mother, even my little cousin who had brought Luke his drink—all began to edge closer. They circled like hungry seagulls. A little blood had sprayed over Opa's face. I smiled at Luke and at last he staggered back from me in revulsion,

as I knew he would. "Your teeth," he stammered.

I licked my elongating canines. "Yep," I said.

"What are you? Are you—oh my god—you're all—"

"What your people made us," I finished. "None of us were like this before the Dutch came, bringing their potatoes and their fob watches and their trade and their monsters. And now look. Look what they made us into." Maybe it was my imagination, but over Luke's shoulder I'm sure I saw Opa's grey eyes glitter.

Luke stumbled backwards, his hip joggling the table laden with food. "This can't be—*real*—" He held out a hand, warding me off, reaching out—I didn't know. I didn't care. "But you—you're not pale, or—"

"Of course not. We're brown people. We don't fit the usual cliches. Same with the garlic thing. Garlic doesn't fend us off. We're from Southeast Asia, we love garlic."

Luke fumbled at his neck and pulled out his crucifix on a silver chain. He tugged it free from his neck and brandished it at me, at my family as they circled him tighter. "Stay back!" he screeched.

"I already told you," I said patiently as I continued to advance. "That Christian shit doesn't work with us." I slashed at him again, enjoying the swing of the blade through the air. The tip of the knife caught his forearm and opened a deep divot. Thick pearls of blood, as if dropped from a pomegranate, welled up. Beautiful.

Luke lost his footing and fell to the floor. Now he was the one who was pale, while his white shirt became more and more white-and-red. He cowered. "Please!" he said. His pupils widened, black with that old familiar fear. "I don't deserve this!"

Deserve? I listened to Luke's panicked gasps, his thundering heart, the tumble of his red blood cells in his carotid. What he deserved was irrelevant. What about what we deserved, 500 years ago? I felt Opa's mind reach out to me, try to say something to me—I caught my name faintly, a feather on the wind—but I blocked out the rest. Stay the course. I would not be weak at the end.

A red pearl hovered on Opa's upper lip. It fell, slid over, and seeped into the crease of his dry blue mouth. He couldn't help it. He licked his lips. Almost instantly, the blue in his lip and fingers retreated. His hunched back straightened. He lifted his head with ease, and I saw his grey eyes gain life and power and pride. Once again, I saw the old Opa, my hero, the Opa who had brought us to this new land, who had carved a home out for us, who had protected and

fed us, who had slaughtered colonisers for our dinner table. His grey eyes brightened with hatred.

For the first time I saw how much I looked like him. His sharp teeth, his anger, his curse. And for the first time, I was afraid.

"Ayo," Opa said. "Makan." Luke screamed. Then we fell on him.

# THE BOOK OF NATURE'S MARVELS

## BY KAARON WARREN

It's a beautiful book.
I found it at the shop where I work, a
second-hand shop
where we get the belongings of dead
people and we sell them to the living.
The book was given as a prize to Cynthia
Clifford, Dow Hill School, Kurseong,
India.
Tucked into the cover of the book were
some handwritten pages.
I'm going to read them to you.

Cynthia Clifford didn't believe she'd ever
find love. She had a skewed idea of what
love was, having grown up a lonely child
with an absent father and a neat-obsessed
mother.

Her mother ran a clothing shop in
Delhi, a dark, cool space filled with suits
and dresses no one would buy, thick
heavy materials, old-fashioned, ugly
designs. Cynthia refused to wear any
of it, but would hack at a dress with the
good scissors until she had something
acceptable. This was in 1938 and such
waste was considered a crime. Certainly
her mother was so angry she sent her away
to school in Darjeeling.

"You can send me tea, dear. Like a good
girl."

So Cynthia packed two suitcases under
her mother's guidance, and she began the
long journey to the school.

Cynthia wondered what would happen if
she refused, or if she simply stayed on the
train, missed the stop and kept going. If
she never arrived at the school.

She'd never be given this book as a prize,
for one.

***

It wasn't a terrible school, although
every day doors slammed when no one
was there, and it sat in the centre of a
dark, forbidding forest. If she walked the
corridors of the girls' dormitory at night,
needing the bathroom, she felt someone
watching her, and in the bathroom
she always put the light on and would
hum, because otherwise she might hear
someone breathing in that dark, empty
space.

No one ever walked the path through
the forest at night, or alone. Cynthia
discovered that it was far darker than it
should be, and there were huts here and
there, collapsed and overrun with vines
and moss, reeking of rot and old wood.
It was always foggy, as were the school
grounds, and if you tripped over a tree
root, you didn't look closely in case it was
a human bone.

If you were bad in this school (and
perhaps it was a terrible school, truth be
told) the teachers would make you sit
alone in a dark room. Your torch wouldn't
work and no one knew why. In the corner
was a rocking chair and, while Cynthia
never saw her, others did: a tall white lady

rocking back and forth, back and forth, thin and flat like paper. Cynthia never saw the headless boy, either, but others told stories of him kicking his own head around like a football. They all loved that story and would act it out.

Scary stories are what kept them happy there, and interested.

It certainly wasn't the food, disappointing British stodge rather than good Indian curries.

Was it deliberate cruelty, Cynthia Clifford's mother sending her to the Dow Hill school?

She won this book in 1940. It would be the only prize she ever won.

This is a very special book, handmade in the town of Kurseong, for the yearly prize giving. Even the paper is handmade, from the trees of the surrounding tall forest.

The smell of an old book
The feel of the pages

The Christmas holidays were lonely for Cynthia the year she won the book. There were only a few girls left at the school; Cynthia's mum wouldn't take her home. It's the busy season, she said.

Cynthia's thinking, why did I even come here? She's thinking, I could be anywhere.

*The Book of Nature's Marvels* sat open on her bedside table.

In the middle of the night, Cynthia was awoken by the sound of pages turning. "Oi! Leave my book alone!" she called, her voice sleepy and slow. She reached out her hand to grab the culprit who wanted to steal her prize book, but felt nothing.

The sound of pages turning, of rustling, increased, and she sat up in bed, blinked her eyes to adjust them to the moonlit room.

She had dust in her eyes, though, motes, because it looked like a man was unfolding himself from the covers of the book. He stretched out, pale and thin, transparent, his features formed of wrinkles in the paper. A scream caught in her throat as he reached for her, and then she released it, waking every girl in the room.

"A man! A man!" The others roused slowly. The paperman turned to watch them all then, as they approached, lightning fast, he slit first this throat then that, five girls collapsed to the floor, heads tipped back like PEZ dispensers, blood black in the moonlight. Others, he reached out his folded arms and wrapped his paper fingers around their young necks.

Cynthia sobbed, terrified, sick with terror. One girl came at him, threw a lit candle at the paperman. It flew straight through him (but how, when his own hand strangled those girls?) and set the bed alight.

The paperman spread his arms as if welcoming the flames. The heat.

The smell of smoke in this book.

Cynthia gathered up the book and leapt out the window. The paperman took her hand and leapt with her, he enfolded her, rested his face, his papery lips on hers. Like her old grandad and his awful bedtime kisses, and she shuddered, and he provided no safety net for her.
A Christmas miracle. This book survived. Cynthia died holding it.

\*\*\*

No doubt who the book belonged to, and why. It was packed up with the sparse rest of her belongings and sent to her mother, sitting amongst the fabric and pins in her small Delhi shop.

The book smelled of smoke and of the forest, an earthy, heady smell. Cynthia's clothing was folded neatly. Her mother gave that to a poor woman on the street. She kept the prize book by the till to show people how proud she was of her poor, dead daughter.

There was a photo in the book, all the girls dressed ready to play a game of sport. It wasn't a happy photo but it was all she had. Some of the girls were blurred, transparent, looking like ghosts.

All of them dead now, every last one.

One evening as she was closing up, a young man pushed his way in. Loud, brash, he demanded some trousers (his, indeed, were beyond repair) and told her he wouldn't pay, that his father was the British Consul and therefore it was all his anyway.

She made the mistake of laughing, realising too late he was perfectly serious. With surprising grace, he snatched up her heavy marble paperweight and clouted her. She fell into a heap, still conscious, unwilling to move or speak.

Through the veil of hair that had fallen into her face, she saw him raise his weapon again.

She heard a rustling sound, like her husband reading The Times at the table on a Sunday. She couldn't stop a cry of shock as, from the book on the counter, what appeared to be a man made out of paper unfolded, broad and tall. His facial features were clear, his expression determined and angry, focussed. He stepped towards

the young man and lifted him by the hair before slamming him against the desk like a washerwoman drying a shirt on rocks at the side of the river.

The young man grunted, and she felt a splattering of liquid, saw his blood pooling around her, and she drew herself up tiny and small.

The paperman bent over and kissed her. "You taste like your daughter," he whispered, before he folded himself back into the book.

That book.

She was cool there on the floor. Almost comfortable.

It was a month before anyone official found her and the young man, and by then, the shop had been stripped bare. Every scrap of material, every pin, the good scissors and bad, the account sheets, even the old brandy she kept in her desk (but not the desk itself).

*Even The Book of Nature's Marvels.*

The photo of Cynthia and her sports team they left, resting it over the woman's heart.

Smell the pages. Can you smell that paperman? He smells of smoke and the forest, of dust, he smells of blood and of the perfume of the women he's kissed. He smells of brandy. He is the conglomeration of all the souls, all who have read and touched the book. He is Cynthia. He is her mother. He is stronger every time.

Maybe the paperman is the muse, the voice, the story on the page. Words that haunt you.

You'll see soon enough, when the paperman unfolds before you.

# MOULDER

## BY EM STARR

It's been forty winters since they buried that time capsule in the out-of-bounds zone at Glenroy State School, and soon the digging will start.

The day is unseasonably hot for mid-August, and Principal West is coveting the shade of the welcome sign, greeting ex-students through a warbled microphone. He's making bad-taste jokes, and none of them are landing, and it feels like 1983 all over again. He scans the meagre crowd for familiar faces, frog-eyed and nervous. I could save him the trouble and tell him she's not coming, but I like to watch him sweat.

I could tell him many things, the silly old fool—speak secrets into his ear-fluff as he gestures to rows of fold-out chairs, in that same old pit-stained shirt, and asks for quiet please. I could tell him Bobby Klein will soon be here and he'll ride the gutter of the drop-off bay in a Commodore with squeaking brakes, and scream at his wife for adjusting the rear-view mirror. That Michael C will run late because the train station is so much further than he remembers. That the Pollard sisters and Tricia Frost just shared a sneaky carafe at their catch-up brunch, and they'll bitch and giggle in the back row, like they did at school assembly.

And none of them will ask about the girl who used to play in the dirt.

I could tell him many things—awful things—if he'd listen, but Principal West has never been good at listening, so I watch him swelter in the midday sun and wait for the sweet scrapings of shovel on soil.

***

She was friends with the bugs and the crawly things, and her dirty fingernails stained the chalk, and that's just one of the reasons nobody wanted to play with her.

"Dirty Gertie! Dirty Gertie!" they'd say, lingering in the canteen line for party pies and Sunnyboys and laughing at the loose cling-wrap that flapped around her vegemite sandwich. She held her breath as she walked by them, hurrying to the garden with air-puffed cheeks so she couldn't smell the pastry and tomato sauce, exhaling only when she could breathe in the musk of sweet, wet dirt. She turned the rocks, one by one, and shared breadcrumbs with the wood lice that crawled underneath. Pretended she couldn't hear the kids still laughing through their meat pie teeth, their pockets fat and jingling with lunch money.

"At least I have you," she said to the bugs, scooping them up, oh-so-gently.

At first, they curled into armoured balls, little rollie-pollies in the palm of her hand, but with patience they always unfurled, and by the time the lunch bell rang there'd be insects exploring the creases of her heartline, her headline, her lifeline. Little grey bugs crawling all over her skin.

"Ewwww, look at Dirty Gertie," the kids would say, five of them worse than the rest. And they never let her play Red Rover, or swing with them on the monkey bars, no matter how much she scrubbed at her fingernails. Tricia and the Pollard twins named the second-last water fountain the Dirty Gertie Bubbler, and nobody drank from it but her, and Bobby and Michael made puking sounds whenever she did, so she spent her days dry and parched and longing for hydration, while they laughed and sucked at chocolate milk.

But that all fell away when she played with her pill bugs—there was comfort in the company of crustaceans, and earthworms and microbes. She sat in the dead leaf mulch, and pretended she lived down there in the dirt, with all her terrestrial friends, where there were no canteens, or monkey bars, and dirty fingernails were the norm.

And I watched her, like a trap-door spider, and decided we should be pals.

***

They're all here now, grouping together on undersized plastic chairs, like their quintet did four decades ago. Bobby's wife sits on the outer and prays there'll be no reunion drinks afterwards, but by the way Jenny Pollard is fingering his shirt collar, we both know she has bigger problems. Principal West is tapping at the microphone as if he doesn't notice the feedback. His sweat stain has spread to his back, the sun far too high in the sky for a Melbourne winter.

"I know we are a little early for this," he says, "But we're building a new gymnasium on this site next year, so we've had to bring things forward."

He makes a bad joke about time-travelling, receives nothing from his disinterested audience, and moves on to the ceremonial bureaucracy, the rehashing of school history and school spirit. Next will be the digging. The unearthing.

Soon they'll be six feet in the ground, ready to exhume that old corpse filled with time and paper scraps and oh! the things they'll find when the trapdoor is opened.

***

The whole school burned with Time Capsule fever for weeks before they buried the thing. They spent their classroom hours discussing the future, talking about who they wanted to be. Bobby said he was going to be a heavyweight boxer, like Rocky, and beat the shit out of his old man… Michael would be his trainer, not his manager, and the dumb kid went along with it, even though he wanted to be a butcher. Tricia drew pictures of herself on the Young Talent Time stage, and Jenny and Jackie dreamed of being gold medal relay-runners at the Commonwealth Games, though neither of them could pass a baton.

Gertie didn't like to think about the future. Forty years was a long time, and her lifeline was short. She forced her mind forward through the decades, and as always, her mind returned to the cold comfort of dirt and earth. She refused to write a letter for the time capsule, and wound up in Principal West's office, where she'd already learned to keep her mouth shut. He had no interest in water bubblers and bullies, he only wondered why she didn't try harder to fit in.

"Why do you have to make things so

difficult, Gertrude?" he said, scratching more red ink onto her school records. "Do I need to call your parents again?"

And he didn't notice the way she cringed as he reached for the phone, how pale she turned when he lifted the receiver from its cradle and threatened to dial. He held it in the air, suggested she think about it over lunchtime, try again. Try harder. She promised she would, and he hung up the phone.

"And wash those fingernails," he said, hurrying her out of the office to attend to the next naughty child. "They're filthy."

And she scrubbed at those nails till the skin on her fingers was raw, confined to the dribbles of the Dirty Gertie Bubbler, willing herself to think forward, to span the decades and see what the future held for her. But all she saw was dirt, all she craved was dirt, and soon she was back in the garden, seeking comfort from slaters and mud. She didn't bring her lunch that day, the last few slices of bread too mouldy to cut away, and the canteen smelled like sausage rolls and finger buns. She wondered what it was like to have a pocketful of loose coins and filled her own with dirt to compare.

She joined the canteen queue, and hoped the lunch ladies would think it was worth something.

"Where's your vegemite sandwich, Dirty Gertie?" they all teased her, but she kept her eyes forward, inching ahead one purchase at a time.

When she finally reached the front of the line, and the aproned lady asked to take her order, she pointed to the pie-warmer, belly screaming as the woman reached for tongs and a brown paper bag and let too many pastry flakes fall to the ground. She carried a meat pie back to the counter, tomato sauce and gravy bleeding through the paper bag, and smiled at Gertie.

"One dollar, thanks, love."

Gertie reached into her pocket, took out a fistful of dirt, plonked it on the counter. It was crawling with ants and spiders that spilled over the counter and into the kitchen, and the Apron Lady screamed. Told her to get out of there. Took back the pie.

Gertie turned away, head down, waited for the jeers to start— Dirty Gertie! Dirty Gertie!—but they never came. She looked up, expecting to see them all staring, and laughing, but none of the usual taunters were there. And when she returned to the garden, she saw someone had overturned the rocks, in her absence, and stomped on all her little friends.

She scooped earth over their broken armours, their roly-poly bodies squashed and squirming, and I whispered condolences to her, as she turned the soil. And I know she heard me, because, when the lunch bell rang, she took a fresh sheet of paper and wrote her piece for the time capsule. Sealed it with dirt and bug guts. Dedicated it to Bobby and Co.

\*\*\*

Curses are a beautiful thing, especially when they're unintentional, accidental, evoked by angry words and innocent minds. When the time capsule was buried, I was already writhing inside it, hungry and sniffing at paper folds and pencil lead. Ready to eat. They've felt me over the years, too, sensed me feeding on the scraps of their dreams, savouring their lost opportunities like mulled wine and blue cheese. Delicious. Each word, each inky hope, devoured in life as I feasted below.

When Bobby lost his punching hand in a factory mincer, his right hook gone in a flurry of meat and red spray, and he kept screaming about the shadow that flicked off the safety switch. That was me.

When Michael was at the bus stop, after losing two large on a horse called Mud, and he thought he saw that monster in the reflection, stooped and sniffing at his hair with a twisted, lupine grin. That was me.

When Tricia Frost fell from her Young Talent Time stage, into studio lights that burned her hair, her face, her career, and she swore that someone shoved her from behind. That was me.

When Jenny and Jackie were dismissed from the State team because they failed the drug test, and neither of them ever touched a banned substance. You best believe that was me.

And now they're all here, and the digging has started, and the best is yet to come.

And when the capsule is pried opened, and they find me coiled amongst the decay and detritus and dead bugs, they might finally ask where Gertie is. As they claw at their faces, and scratch at their eyes, and scream her name till their lungs turn ashy, I'll tell them she lives down here with me now. That she likes how the bugs move through her bones, how the worms writhe in her eye sockets, how the earth fills her belly.

That we love the dirt, she and I, and we are old friends.

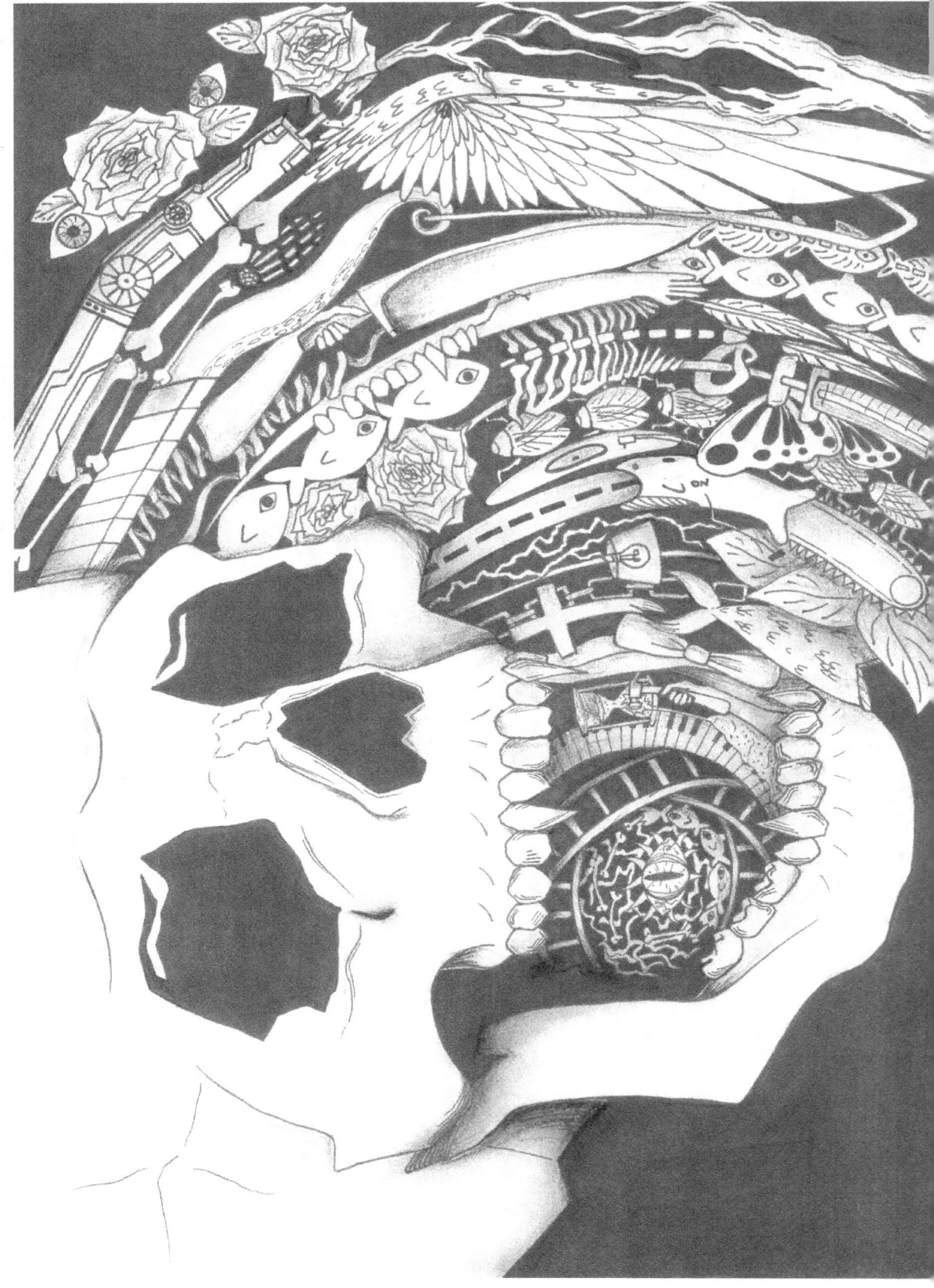

DREAMSPARKLE

# BY BRENT McGREGOR

"Well, don't stand there gaping you, idiot, get over here and help," Betty said.

Ned hustled to take the box from his wife. "Sorry, darling. Where do you want it?"

"Just put it with the others." She gestured to a stack of mover's boxes in the corner.

Betty shook out the tension in her wrists, surveying the mess that was the kitchen. *Oh God, it's hideous.* She hated everything about it, from the linoleum floor and laminate counters; to the avocado green splashbacks and yellow, patterned wallpaper. *What did I do in a past life to deserve this?*

She checked her cell phone in case there was a message from her tennis coach, anything to cheer her up.

"Look, I don't want to fight, okay?" Ned smoothed his tie. Dressed for work and with his wire frame glasses he bore more than a passing resemblance to Bill Gates.

Betty eyed his paunch. All through college—thanks to a lucky metabolism—he'd been lank and sinewy, but he'd packed on the pounds in recent years. "You always do this," she said. "I could have used your help cleaning and unpacking. You're not pitching in."

Ned winced. "It's not like I have a choice, darling. It's a new job."

Betty shook her head. It wasn't a new job, not really. Ned had been passed over for a promotion at the bank, then got himself transferred to a different branch—which was as good as a demotion in her eyes. They'd been forced to sell their beautiful apartment in town, trading it in for a postmodern fixer-upper in the suburbs.

She felt an all too familiar throbbing behind her eyes and pinched the bridge of her nose. It was probably a migraine. "Will you hurry? You've got to drop Alex at school, remember?"

"Oh jeez. Is that today?" Ned said, rubbing the back of his neck.

Their seven-year-old, Alex, sat at the breakfast nook eating Corn Flakes from an oversized bowl, watching them from beneath his shaggy fringe.

"Morning, kiddo." Ned ruffled the boy's hair. "You ready for your first day of school?"

"Not really," Alex said, munching.

"That's the spirit." Ned swiped a slice of toast.

"It's not my first day of school, Dad."

"We know that, chief," Ned said. "But it is your first day at a new school, and first impressions count." He ate the slice of toast before putting his jacket on. "You ready to go?"

Alex nodded.

On their way out, Ned leaned in to kiss his wife goodbye, but she shifted her head so he only managed to peck her cheek. He lingered for a moment before shuffling—

with Alex in tow—in the direction of their lime-green Mazda parked in the driveway.

"Oh, Ned," Betty called out. "Did you contact the electricity company yet, to let them know we've moved?"

"Uh-huh. Yes, dear," he said, strapping Alex into the booster seat.

"What about Telstra?"

"The what?" Ned said, shutting the door on the passenger-side.

"The telephone company…to connect the phone?"

"Right—of course," he said putting palm to forehead. "I'll get right on it."

Betty watched them back out the driveway and disappear up the street.

\*\*\*

A short while later, Betty slid an idle hand over the kitchen counter, appalled at the thin layer of grease she found there. It was filthy, a veritable history of food preparation. *No point in putting things away yet. This all needs cleaning.* And she slid the packing boxes into the living room—but not before shifting the ugly macramé lamp Ned's mother had bequeathed them a year earlier.

*What am I getting myself in for?*

While examining the sink—which was noxious-smelling, and covered with lime scale—she gave an involuntary shudder. 'There's more faecal bacteria in your sink than a flushed toilet,' she remembered hearing once. Still, she was surprised at the level of scum around the drain and in the crevices where the sink joined the counter.

The stove was an ancient-looking thing from General Electric, with a collection of knobs and dials more reminiscent, perhaps, of the Apollo 11 Space Module than a kitchen appliance. All its markings

were worn-off, and the stovetop was foul with animal fat and cooking oil.

The bathroom, too, was a haven for all manner of putrescence. The toilet bowl was covered in grime and the bathtub had a dirty, brown halo.

She sighed deeply and put on rubber gloves. *Fuck my life. I hitched my wagon to the wrong horse.* She had loved Ned once, back when they were first married; he was laid-back, affable. But somewhere along the way they'd lost that spark.

Betty opened the fridge and cracked a cranberry wine cooler. It was early but this had never stopped her before. What was it that killed the spark, she wondered. The sex? Maybe. Ever since he'd gained the weight she wasn't attracted to him anymore. She'd feigned more than her fair share of headaches. *That isn't the real reason, though, is it? Nope.* She took a gulp of wine cooler. *You know what it is? He lacks motivation.*

Her mother was right. "He'll never be successful," she used to say. "He'll never amount to anything." It was true. Ned was supremely ungifted. Awkward. Ungainly.

She took another gulp of her wine cooler. He'd led them into one dumb financial decision after another, and that's why, now, they were living in this three-bedroom dive.

*Where did life go so wrong? I wasn't the most popular kid in high school but I wasn't unpopular.* She cursed under her breath. *I could have married Tim Dorsey from high school. He owns his own tech company. Probably owns his own Island, too.*

She sipped at her wine cooler, and thought of Jane, her girlfriend from book club. *Why couldn't I have married someone like Jane's husband, Andrew?* He's an entrepreneur. *He owns his own line of gas stations. He has a lucrative investment portfolio. I bet he doesn't drive a second-hand Mazda.*

She deserved better. She launched her empty at the bin. *That's why I don't feel guilty for sleeping around. Would Ned even care if he knew? Yes, but it wouldn't change anything. I'm not having my needs met. This thing with Mike, it isn't love or anything, just fucking. The truth is, before the affair, I felt kind of aimless, bored. Screwing Michael Foster—even if he is a better tennis coach than he is a lover—has made everything bearable. So, no, I don't feel guilty. Call it payback for allowing me to live in this squalor.*

While clearing under the sink, Betty moved a bundle of rags, which released a scuttle of silverfish. She squealed, squashing each of them.

After regaining her composure, she found, at the back of the cupboard, several dusty, piles of interior decorating magazines. They had titles like *Beautiful Homes*, and *Simply Vogue*. In addition, there was a box of something called DreamSparkle. "Lord, how long has this been here?" She said aloud, setting the box aside.

Flicking through several of the magazines, Betty thought that, perhaps, the previous owner had been one of these hoarder-types, seeing there were issues dating back decades. Turning the yellowed pages felt like stepping back in time. There were pictures of elegant dining rooms, stylish lounge rooms, luxurious bedrooms, and traditional kitchens. There was an abundance of furniture with fancy-sounding names: gainsboroughs, chesterfields, armoires, and chaise lounges.

Indeed, as she thumbed the pages, she saw the fashions change from the bold abstract designs of the 50s and 60s; to the funky and psychedelic prints of the 70s; and the pastel colours of the 80s. Throughout were the usual series of display ads—for cosmetics, women's fashion, steak knives, and cleaning products.

One ad caught Betty's attention in particular, though, and that was an ad for DreamSparkle. Her eyes darted to her own box of the product before returning to the page. It was a full-page ad, showing an apron-adorned woman, standing in her kitchen, beaming a happy smile, a box of DreamSparkle in one hand, making a sort of voila-there-you-have-it gesture with the other. Betty raised an eyebrow. She flicked through the other magazines. *Strange, that the same ad should be in every issue.* It was the same ad, except the fashions of the woman, like the background, seemed to change through the years; from a pencil skirt with a bouffant hairstyle to blue jeans and a Farrah Fawcett do. *You'd think they'd vary the ad a little*, she thought. *That's just lazy advertising.*

She read the ad aloud, mimicking an infomercial-type voice. "DreamSparkle, Australia's number one disinfectant, and household grade cleaner, cleans bathroom and kitchen surfaces faster. Now with Forest Rain Scent." Again she eyed her own box of DreamSparkle.

"Worth a try I guess, " she said, shrugging and opening the box. She caught a whiff of forest flowers.

Following the directions on the back, she sprinkled the powder over the surface of the kitchen counter. Then, with a wet cloth, she rinsed. The mixture instantly fizzled, hissed, and bubbled.

"Oh wow! Is it supposed to do that?" she exclaimed, before turning the box over and ready the warning label:

KEEP OUT OF REACH OF CHILDREN
AVOID CONTACT WITH SKIN
CALL 1-800-975-708 IMMEDIATELY
FOR TREATMENT ADVICE

"Good to know." She put the box down. It was miraculous stuff, amazing, and it cleaned faster than other products.

First, she used DreamSparkle to clean the kitchen counters, wiping away the layers of grease and muck until they shone, immaculate. *How can I sustain myself in this loveless marriage? I feel like I'm in a vacuum without air. But I need to breathe. Do I still love, Ned? I don't know if I do.*

Then she moved to the kitchen sink. The mixture, again, fizzled, hissed, and bubbled. She scrubbed away the scum and grime, being careful to clean out the crevices where all those microorganisms could get trapped. *I've felt this way for a while. All this sneaking around. Avoiding getting caught. It makes me feel dirty.* She polished vigorously until the sink was brilliant and glowing.

Moving to the stove she used DreamSparkle to eliminate the copious food stains, soot, and food debris until everything was spick-and-span.

In the bathroom, she scrubbed the sink and toilet until they were both spotless and shiny-white. *I'm honest enough to admit I'm not happy. In fact, if I have to take one more night of Ned's awkward lovemaking I think I might scream.*

Betty used DreamSparkle on the bathtub, too, washing away the brown halo, erasing successive years of dirt and bacteria, until the tub was fresh and glowing. *I mean what's keeping me here? Not a lot, right? This shitty dive? A roof over our heads?*

*Maybe I should pack my bags and Alex and I can go live with Michael for a while. Michael's an idiot but I prefer his company to Ned's. In fact, I think I will call Michael. Fuck it! I'll call him, now. I'll pack our bags tonight. Then, in time, maybe I'll file for divorce. Maybe even get my own little apartment in town.*

Betty pulled the tab on another wine cooler. It was already midday. She hiccupped. It always took her 'til her second or third to get a sufficient buzz going.

Returning to the kitchen, she stepped over the pile of magazines, setting the box of DreamSparkle on the counter. She removed her rubber gloves.

*Da-amn!* She looked around, tired, but impressed with her own handy work. *This place is looking cleaner. But hopefully, I won't have to stomach it too much longer.*

She took her cell phone from her pocket and started texting Michael—who was in her phone as Magic Mike.

"*Hey,*" she typed.

She waited. Three dots came up on the screen indicating that he was texting back.

"*Hey, yourself,*" he replied, adding the suggestive winky-face-emoji.

"*Can I crash at yours' tonight—I'll have Alex with me?*"

"*Sure. Is everything okay?*"

She started texting but her cell phone screen went black.

"Shit!" She threw her cell on the counter. What a time for the battery to go flat — and she had no idea which box the charger was in.

Tilting her head, she drained the last of

her drink before discarding the empty.

She tried the landline phone next but didn't hear a dial tone. "Fucking, Ned," she hissed, slamming the phone on the cradle. "Still hasn't called the phone company."

*Screw it.* She made towards the fridge to get yet another wine cooler. Only, her foot slipped on one of the glossy magazine covers and she started to fall. Time seemed to move in slow motion. Had she been sober, she could have stopped herself—but she wasn't and didn't. She grasped at whatever she could, upsetting the box of DreamSparkle on the counter. She fell hard against the kitchen cabinets, then flat on the linoleum floor. Staring up at the ceiling light, she saw the box of DreamSparkle tilt and fall, releasing its corrosive, powder contents. There was a puff of white cloud and it was all over her, coating her face and chest, arms, and thighs.

"Oh, God! It burns! It burns!" she screamed, arms flailing. She closed her eyes then opened them. They stung like a son-of-a-bitch. Her vision blurred and the world was a kaleidoscope of smudgy shapes. She staggered to her feet, knocking over the macramé lamp.

*I'll wash it off.* She willed herself to the bathroom, where, she stripped to her underwear and jumped under the shower. The water didn't relieve the pain, though, or stop the burning. In fact, it made it worse. The water ran hard and the spray hurt horribly.

She was shocked when she looked at her own hands. They'd lost the upper layers of dermis and were pink and bloodied, emaciated, like something out of *Night of the Living Dead*. Between her feet, she saw the water mix with blood—and bits of what? To her horror, she realized they were pieces of her own skin. Her hands went to her arms and chest, and then to her face. She didn't recognize their features. Where they were once smooth and soft, they were, now, rough and textured. *My God, why is it still burning?*

"Oh no, no, no, no," she said, making a pathetic whimper-like sound.

*Is the whole world on fire?*

After getting out, she looked in the mirror and screamed, for, the thing staring back at her, her own reflection, was unrecognizable. It was her, but then again wasn't. Her scalp was mottled, and exposed. Her hair, once long and beautiful had fallen out. Her lips had corroded, turning her mouth into a terrifying, toothy grin.

It was still burning, though, and she could feel DreamSparkle's chemicals eating deeper and deeper into her dermis like she was the incredible melting woman.

"Help me!" she yelled, running back to the kitchen, hoping the neighbours might hear.

*I need to do something. It's killing me.* She remembered the magazine ad. *'Call blankety-blank for treatment advice.'*

She fell to her knees and began, frantically, flicking through the magazines, the corners of the pages sticking to her bloody fingertips. Eventually, she found what she was looking for. The ad was still there of course, with the woman wearing the apron, with that same beaming happy smile, with that same voila-there-you-have-it gesture, but it was different somehow. *What was different?* She didn't care. She had the number for the treatment line.

Betty stood up, panicked, the magazine still in hand. She picked up the handset and started dialling. While bashing the numbers with one bloody digit, she realized there was no dial tone. Ned still hadn't called the phone company.

*Fuck!* It dawned on her she wouldn't be calling anyone, and she sank to her knees, letting the handset hang from its cord.

Looking at the magazine again, she noticed why the ad had been so different. *What the fuck?* One side of the DreamSparkle woman's face was red and burned, her mouth, a twisted and bloody maw.

Betty opened another magazine to see if the ad had changed there, too, and it had. She opened another, and another, until she had scrutinized every single one.

They were all different. They'd all changed. But how? Each and every single ad was horrific, showing the apron-adorned DreamSparkle woman, stepping away from their kitchens in various degrees of disintegration, with hideous burns—and it got worse in the later issues. It was like a demented flick book, showing the progressively worsening states of decomposition.

*Who put these magazines here? Is this some kind of sick practical joke?* But then something occurred to her she hadn't noticed before. It wasn't just the same woman in all of the DreamSparkle ads; it was, also, the same kitchen. In fact, it was *her* kitchen. She looked about her—at the counter, the sink, at the kitchen cabinets—and knew it was true.

*Oh Jesus. I'm the woman in the ad.*

"Help!" she screamed, slumping against the kitchen cabinets. "Oh, God, please."

*I'm sorry.* She clutched her burning chest. *I'm sorry I ever slept with Mike Foster. I wished I'd never even heard his name.* The pain was coming in waves, and she knew the final tsunami would be coming soon.

*I love you, Ned. I was a fool not to have realized it. The more I think about it…I've never not loved you.* Her breathing grew laboured. *You and Alex. Oh, my beautiful baby.*

She cried more and more bloody tears. *Wait, what will they think when they come home and find me, or, what's left of me, a melted and bloody mess?*

She laughed a strange sort of laugh, and wondered if, perhaps, she'd already lost the grip on her sanity.

*Nothing a little DreamSparkle can't fix.*

# SIREN SONG

## BY DMITRI AKERS

The siren song resounds above the storm

Amidst the clash and clang of thunder's might,

As tenebrous obscene things come and form

Above the dying light of welkin's height,

The shades begin to grow into insane

And dreadful horrors in the spectral light

With piercing squalls above the earthly plane

To madly wail and dance, to siren-sung refrain:

They fall to earth beneath an elder sign

And change into a troupe of minstrel beasts,

A drumming beat intoxicates as wine,

And corpses char and cook for awful feasts

To feed the shambling pipers who cavort

And drink the blood of vines with pungent yeasts

Inside their Bacchic glee and horrid rort

Of revelled ecstasy, at such a maddened court.

So, when you hear the siren's song so foul

To piping crescendo and maddened drum,

Remember how accursed things come and howl

The curses from beyond—and dead we shall become.

# INTO THE FIRE

## BY CHRIS MASON

A guy called Wendell King owned Semaphore Studios. He'd converted an old boarding house into a rabbit warren of band practice rooms upstairs and a recording studio in the basement. Wendell looked like a ferret and didn't shower much, but he'd inherited some coin from his father to buy the place and was an aficionado of all things rock'n'roll. If you let him, he could talk for hours about how if it wasn't for his carpal tunnel he could have been in Thin Lizzy. Or Black Sabbath. Or Jethro Tull. Take your pick. His rates were cheap though. For two hundred bucks a band could get the entire studio for the night with the only proviso everything would be bumped out by eight the next morning.

I met Wendell in 1977 when I was eighteen. In my final year of school, I'd joined a band. Andy, the guitarist, had heard me yelling in class and thought my voice might work with what he had in mind. He was putting together a five-piece rock outfit—drums, bass, two guitars, vocals—and thought it'd be a good idea to have a big-haired, big-voiced girl out front. I had a mane of tangles plus a set of lungs I wasn't afraid to use. It probably helped I bore a resemblance to Kate Bush, could match Ronnie James Dio's range, and had every album Uriah Heep had put out. Besides hating school, Andy and I

had one thing in common; we dreamed of being rock stars. Once I said I was in, it didn't take long to find the others. Gareth, the drummer, came to us via Biology class, and Matt, the second guitarist, by way of a suspension. He'd been caught lighting farts in the boy's toilets and was given two weeks to get his act together which meant he had ample time to sit in his room and practice on his *Ibanez*. Tommy, our bass player was the outsider. A year older than the rest of us, he lived next door to Matt and hadn't found a job yet. We called ourselves Dark Matter and within a month we had enough songs for our first gig—a lunchtime concert in the school quadrangle. Our careers stalled temporarily when the principal pulled the plug on the PA after the first song—a cover version of *School's Out*. He'd been expecting something more akin to Elvis or Roy Orbison when we'd said we were a rock band. It didn't help that the windows in the staff room shook every time Gareth hit the kick drum (or Matt deciding to perform shirtless, which earned him another two days of suspension).

We got more discerning with the gigs we took—backyard twenty-firsts and engagement parties, football clubs, underage discos. Gareth's dad also found us a regular gig at his local. We played to the barman, a bunch of bikers, and a half-blind blue healer every Tuesday night for a year. We got better and we wrote a heap of songs. It was the era of prog rock and fifteen-minute guitar solos. I provided the lyrics and melody lines, gave the songs some structure, while Andy came up with the riffs and screaming solos. The other boys filled in the rest. Don't ask me how, but it worked.

By the summer of '76 we were hiring bigger PAs and had a road crew—Matt's two younger brothers. Gareth found a tech guy called Benny who for a small supply of weed sat behind a mixing desk and pretended to be cool. Without even trying, he managed to make my vocals flat, the drums tinny and the bass boomy. Turned out no matter what a stoned tech will try to tell you, a ton of reverb won't fix the problem. We replaced him with Rod who knew the difference between a tweeter and a woofer and made us sound like we weren't playing in a garden shed. It was about then an agent took us on with the promise of booking gigs that paid. These all turned out to be in small country towns where the crowds didn't much appreciate our artistic vision and tended to drink and fight a lot. We played in front bars where beer-soaked carpets sparkled with broken glass. Not quite 'chicken wire' territory but close. We toughened up, quick. We got more gigs and punters rolled up. Every now and then someone listened. Somewhere in amongst it all I fell in love with the bass player. Never a good idea.

Eventually, the band attracted the attention of a rep from EMI who told us he liked what we did and if we could get a demo to him, he'd pass it up the line. One song was all he needed. We were good. We only had to prove it. And that's how we ended up at Wendell's.

***

The moment I walked into the studio the place creeped me out. The band had played in some dodgy places, but the basement was on a whole other level. There were no windows for starters and the flickering fluorescent lighting created a trippy vibe more suitable for a live show than a recording session. The control booth had a battered sofa along the back wall, a bar fridge which didn't work, two racks of dusty equipment, and a mixing desk set in front of a big glass window. Beyond was a cavernous recording space where stained egg cartons lined the walls. Filthy carpet offcuts covered the floor. In the back was an improvised drum booth made from old blankets strung over upended pallets. The far corners were unlit, full of boxes and shadows. On the ceiling someone had painted a mural. A frenzy of stars and lines radiating out from a black hole. *Or was it an eye?* I wasn't sure if it was an artistic nod to the cosmos or the result of some bad acid. Either way it was disturbing. No sane hand could have done it. An odour of rat piss and sweet leaf permeated the place.

After wasting more time than we wanted listening to Wendell's stories about his close association with icons of the rock industry, Rod got a five-minute tour of the mixing desk—a sixteen-track analogue antique.

"Used one before?" Wendell asked.

"Yeah," said Rod. He twiddled with a few sliding knobs and checked the tape decks.

Wendell sniffed back a bucketful of phlegm then put his hand out. "Two things before I go. Don't wreck the joint. And I want my money now."

Andy gave him the two hundred.

"There's plenty of power, but the wiring is shit so try not to burn the place down." Wendell grinned. Good to know I'd be spending the next twelve hours in a fire trap.

It took close to an hour for the boys to bump in. Getting all our gear down the narrow stairs wasn't easy. Once the amps and drumkit were in, Rod mic'd everything up. The next hour was spent on finding leads that worked and getting the sound levels right.

Close to midnight we put down a bed track and guide vocal on one of our new songs 'Into the Fire'. I'd written the rock ballad a few weeks before—a break-up song about me and Tommy. Our short time exploring each other had been intense and ultimately a mistake. I'm not sure if we weren't right for each other or not ready. Tommy was a big mystery to me. After eight months of sleeping with him I'd been no closer to working out who he was or what he wanted out of our relationship. The end of my first big love affair gave me something to write about. I poured all the hurt, anger, and pain into the lyrics. 'Into the Fire' was as bitter as they get.

I ran the song by Andy first. He took a minute then said. "Wow. That's a lot. Maybe it's too much. Is Tommy okay with this?"

Tommy listened through to the solo before giving me a lazy one-eyed blink and the smallest of smiles. He waited until I almost apologized, then said, "Good song. We should record it." The art always came first for him.

We took a vote. Everyone agreed. 'Into the Fire' was, despite, or maybe because of, the personal confessions, our best chance of commercial success.

Gareth and Tommy went to work on their bass and drums tracks first. Once everyone was happy with how the rhythm section sounded, Matt went in and put his guitar track down. Next, Andy did his bit and added in the solos. There was a lot of faffing around in between. We didn't get to my vocals until after three in the morning. By then the excitement had worn off. No-one had told me the music business would involve so much sitting around.

As soon as it was my turn to step inside the recording room, I felt panicky. Maybe I was tired. I didn't think it was nerves. On stage I know I can deliver a solid vocal. But this room was different. When I made a sound, the air had no bounce to it. It was if all those egg cartons were sucking the timbre out of my voice. And worse, the mural overhead created a weird energy to the place. Like I was floating among those awful painted stars, while the eye of a leviathan watched over me. The mural hadn't bothered the boys, they'd thought it cool. But then the filth and likelihood of rodents living in the walls hadn't seemed to bother them either. Go figure.

I didn't need to be reminded there was a lot riding on the session and the demo tape. All I needed to do was the main vocal track plus add some harmonies in after. Then I could get the fuck out of there. I asked myself what Suzi Quatro would do and decided she'd be a professional, stop overthinking, and go for it. It didn't help. My first take was a disaster.

I stared at the floor while my brain skipped around all over the place. I wanted to cry. What is wrong with me? I stretched my jaw, my skin all goosebumps. The room was messing with my head. I ran up and down a couple of octaves then turned off the fluoros in favour of a floor lamp with a red shade. The mural faded into shadow, less ominous without the white light picking out every detail, but the space behind me was now a dark void. I tried not to think about the basement where Wendell probably buried body parts in the crawl space under the floor. I imagined ghosts in every corner. Something wet and other-worldly slithering around behind the egg cartons. *Get it together.* I couldn't afford distractions.

On the second try, Rod waved his arms and stopped me halfway through the chorus. "Hang on, I'm coming in," he said through the speakers.

The boys yawned at me through the glass. Matt and Gareth passed a joint between them. Tommy stuck to his bottle of bourbon.

"Think I'm picking up the snare rattling." Rod adjusted the kit, checked nothing else was vibrating and returned to the control booth.

"Let's go again," he said. I slurped on my rum and coke and gave him a thumbs up.

I gave up after the second verse. No one had to tell me the vocals were lacklustre.

Rod leaned forward into the mic. "What's up?"

"I'm cold." It was a lame excuse.

The booth mic off, Andy and Tommy joined Rod in discussion behind the glass. There were a few nods then Tommy took off his suede jacket and brought it in.

"It's not that cold," he said, handing me the jacket. "Must be you." He cast his eyes towards the floor, hesitating. "You want to know the reason I slept with Imogen? It was because I wanted to. I like her." The words came out, rushed.

I glared at him. "Seriously, you want to do this *now?*"

Tommy looked up, his jaw set. "Why not? You're just wasting your time in here." He waited a beat then said, "I don't love you. I never did. If it wasn't Imogen, it would have been someone else. Anyone but you."

"Go to hell." I slammed my hand into his chest.

He grabbed my wrist and held it. "Say it again."

"I hate you. Go burn in hell."

Tommy looked me dead in the eye. "Good. If you're gonna write a lyric like 'Into the Fire', you better sing it like you *fucking mean it*. Keep the jacket."

He returned to the booth, and I watched him reach for the bourbon. It felt like he'd ripped the wound wide open again.

I threw every curse I could think of at him. I didn't care who heard it. I wanted Tommy dead.

Rod disappeared with Matt and Gareth while I vented. Andy sat on the couch beside Tommy, trying his best to not look my way.

"Everything okay in there?" asked Rod when he returned ten minutes later.

I took a breath. "Yeah, I'm good. Let's do this."

He gave me a count in, and in the cold dark space of Wendell's basement I delivered the best damn vocal of my life. Every word hit like an emotional sledgehammer. The high notes were all in there. The tone was raw and edgy, didn't sound contrived like before. It wasn't a performance. Instead, it was as close to the truth as I'd ever get. *Vulnerable.* To be honest, I'm not sure how I managed it. Maybe the stars above had worked their magic. Maybe I had harnessed the dizzy madness of the mural. Or maybe Tommy was an A-grade arsehole, who for all the wrong reasons managed to bring out the best in me.

I took a short break then reluctantly asked Tommy in for our harmonies. He was all business this time. Like our earlier conversation hadn't happened.

His voice carried a lot more soul than mine. He'd listen to a lot of James Brown. I liked the blend our voices created. It was the one thing we still had that was good together. "You want to go again?" I asked after the first take.

"Only if you want to." He grinned but his jaw muscle twitched ever so slightly.

Rod tapped on the glass to get our attention. "Hey, you gotta come listen to this."

\*\*\*

A low growl started in at the thirty second mark. Snippets of my earlier rant followed, garbled into the background.

"What the fuck?" I stared at Rod. "You recorded me while I was having my meltdown?"

He stopped the tape. "I didn't."

"Keep playing," said Andy.

Rod hit the playback button. The growl continued with the verbal vomit fading behind it. Near the end of the solo the screaming began. It continued for a good minute after the end of the song. Then…

*Tommy's dead. Tommy's dead. Tommy's dead. Tommy's dead. Tommy's dead.*

We listened with our mouths open. The tape hissed to a stop.

"This is out of control," said Tommy. He turned to Andy. "You sent me in there to push her buttons, and this is what you do?"

"This has nothing to do with me," said Rod.

"He's right. And no one else went near the desk," said Andy. He turned to Tommy. "You were in here with me, remember? Rod went for a piss. Matt and Gareth were upstairs. You and I sat on the couch while Sharon spat the dummy."

Rod put his palms up. "I have no idea how it could have happened. It's like Sharon's voice has been spliced into the background. As for the rest—"

"This is some weird shit, man," said Matt. "I don't know, but the screaming sounds more like you, Tommy. You got some chops, buddy."

I thought Tommy was going to punch him. "You think this is funny?"

"No one said it was," said Andy.

"Hold on," said Rod. "Let me try and figure this out." He slid every channel off except for the harmonies. We listened to our voices in isolation. Nothing but me and Tommy. Next, Rod brought up my solo vocal. It was fine. He went through all the tracks he'd recorded one by one, separating them out to confirm they were also uncorrupted. When he finally played all the tracks together, wild sounds poured through the speakers along with the sinister message.

"I don't understand," said Rod, shaking his head. "How is this possible?"

I glanced into the big room beyond the glass and for a moment I thought I saw something in the gloom of the far corner. A shape, darker than the shadows surrounding it, tumbling in mid-air. I squinted not understanding what it could be. It seemed vaguely human, all arms and legs, the head at a funny angle. Trembling, I leaned forward and grabbed the desk.

"Something is in there." I pointed.

"What?" asked Rod.

"I don't know."

"I don't see anything," said Rod.

"Andy? Matt? Gareth?"

They all shook their heads.

"Are you shitting me?" said Tommy. Before anyone could stop him, he stormed into the other room. He flicked the fluoro lighting on and checked every corner, pulling aside flight cases and boxes stacked against the back wall.

"Nothing. No one's here." He turned back towards the control room, and I gasped.

In the flickering light, his face was the colour of ash and swollen. The eye with the lazy blink was missing. So was most of his hair. *Tommy?* I looked away and burst into tears.

"What? Can you still see it?" asked Andy.

I squeezed my eyes shut and opened them again. Tommy stood in the middle of the room. He was every bit as perfect as the first day I'd met him.

"No." Had it been a reflection? An hallucination? "I guess I'm tired."

Andy frowned like he wasn't buying it. "If there was something there, it'd explain what's on the tape," he said. "Maybe we've got ourselves a ghost down here."

Had I seen a ghost though? Or something else. Tommy's future? The very thing I'd wished for him when I'd sung my heart out. The thought made me shiver.

"Or maybe it's Wendell dicking around with us," said Rod.

"I can smell smoke," said Matt, joining Tommy on the other side of the glass. "Anyone else?"

The walls creaked and a cymbal stand fell over. We all jumped.

It was Rod who said what we were all

thinking. "I've had enough. Let's pack up and get out of here." He didn't wait for an answer. Instead, he wound back the tape, took it off the spool and put it into a metal can.

The boys bumped out in record time.

\*\*\*

A few days later, and at his own expense, Rod bought time at another studio with the intention of mastering the tape. He called us as soon as he got started. There was a problem. The tape was now 'infected' across all the tracks. What had been good instrumental recordings were now a mess. Time signatures were all over the place. Gareth's drum track switched between seven-eight and twelve-eight time, a feat he could only dream of pulling off, and a long way from the standard four-four he'd put down. Tommy's bassline was like a waltz on crack. Matt's power chords carried so much sustain it was as if Benny was in charge again. And Andy's solo was plain crazy, a manic mix between a Hungarian minor scale and an Oriental with so many bended notes and harmonics it was disturbing. Nothing like he'd recorded… or was even capable of. What sounded like screeching tyres, slowed to about 20 rpm, had now been added to the harmony track.

My vocals were something else. Beyond the first verse, they certainly weren't mine.

I voted to burn the tape.

\*\*\*

Tommy left the band the next day. Said he was sick of our bullshit. He didn't speak to me. He seemed to think he'd been set up and I was complicit. The boys didn't challenge him or ask him to stay. They were more loyal to me than Tommy had ever been. Or maybe they figured it was easier to replace a belligerent bass player than a good singer.

Pissed because we had nothing to give to the EMI rep, Rod and Andy paid Wendell a visit. He was evasive when questioned about the possibility of something supernatural in his studio. All he'd let on was, there was a lot of things wrong with the old building. Nothing would surprise him. At any rate, we weren't getting our money back.

For a while Tommy burned bright. He got his own band together, same line-up except he put himself front and centre doing the lead vocals as well as playing bass. His band ended up with the EMI contract. He put out an album (no hint of me in any of his songs) which in turn lead to support gigs for the big touring bands. Me and the boys returned to our regular Tuesday nights in the front bar of the Hawker Tavern before giving up on the dream completely. I took a base grade clerk position in the public service. Andy went to uni and studied accounting. Matt and Gareth drifted off into their own suburban nightmares. Rod disappeared altogether.

\*\*\*

"Tommy's dead," said Andy.

I sucked in a long slow breath. Exhaled. Fought back tears and nodded.

"I know it's late, but thought it'd be better coming from me than hearing it on the news in the morning."

"Thanks. Come on in." I ushered him into my small apartment. "Do the others know?"

Andy shook his head. "Not yet. They'll be shocked when they hear, but I was more worried about you."

"It's been a long time." Six years. Six years

and not one word from Tommy. "How did it happen?" I asked.

"Car accident."

"Shit."

He sighed. "Yeah but…"

"What is it?"

"You're not going to like this."

I knew what was coming. What I'd been dreading ever since I'd thrown curses at Tommy in Wendell's basement.

Andy drew me into a hug, held me there for a minute then let go. "The car he was in rolled over on the Sturt Highway. Tommy and his crew were on their way back from a gig in Canberra. He was asleep in the back seat. Got thrown around and pinned under the car. The driver and other guy managed to crawl free."

"And?"

He rubbed his chin. His eyes locked on mine. "The car went up in flames, Sharon. They couldn't get him out."

The room spun and Andy wrapped his arms around me again, stopped me from falling.

"It was on the recording," I whispered. "We all heard it."

Later, as he was leaving, Andy said, "It was my idea. Tommy didn't want to do it."

I knew exactly what he was referring too. I'd given it a lot of thought over the years. It had been a cruel trick, to get me to sing like that. Had it not been for Wendell's studio, and what had happened after, it might have delivered the contract we were so desperate to get.

"For what it's worth, Tommy felt bad about fucking up. With Imogen. He knew he'd thrown away a good thing with you."

I didn't want to talk about it.

\*\*\*

I still have Tommy's jacket. His cigarettes

are in the pocket. I can still smell *him* in the lining. Fifty years on and I keep in regular contact with Andy, and funnily enough Rod appeared on my doorstep a few days back. He'd been out of the country since Tommy's death and wanted to come home. Cancer had made him nostalgic. The three of us went out to dinner and we talked to the wee hours about the old band… and Wendell (overdosed in '92). But mainly we talked about Tommy. Rod raised the question, why out of the five of us, Tommy had been marked in the studio that day. I have an idea. There was something in Wendell's basement, something powerful, and I got its attention. When I poured my heart out, it had listened. And when Tommy left the studio, it had followed.

Andy raised the question of why my curse on Tommy took so long. I think the real question is why the universe saw fit to do my bidding. I'm nobody. And since the building Wendell owned was pushed down a decade ago, the mystery of the mural and the force I unleashed will have to go unsolved. But what I do know is this, words have power. I should have kept my mouth shut and not taken the bait. Tommy might still be alive.

*Tommy's dead. Tommy's dead. Tommy's dead. Tommy's dead. Tommy's dead.*

Even now I hear him screaming. It's like tinnitus. It'll never go away.

## SMILEY FRANK

## BY MATTHEW SCOTT

The movie was over, but neither Bradley nor Hayden wanted to go home just yet. Town was just starting to liven up, and if they hung around outside the Hazard Zone for long enough they might be able to convince an 18-year-old to buy them some Diesel cans.

Besides, the movie was lame anyway—they'd spent most of the time throwing Jaffas at the screen until an usher came and shoved a torchlight in their faces. After that they'd dutifully sat on their hands and watched the car chases and the explosions and the heroic sacrifice at the last minute that turned out not to be much of a sacrifice after all.

There was never anything good on. But still, there wasn't much else to do in Vinetown on a wet and windy July evening in the school holidays. There were probably some raging parties in barns on the outskirts of town, or in flats in the Avenues, but they were too young and too unnoticed to know where to RSVP.

So they wandered down Cameron Street mall, looking in dark shop windows. Bradley always felt like he was being watched from the shadows.

"You could do a smash and grab so easy at this time of night," Hayden said. "Just need a getaway."

"Alright, you smash, I'll grab," Bradley said.

"Far, I knew you'd be keen," Hayden said. "But nah, we'll have to wait until I get my license."

He'd promised he'd be able to borrow his dad's Toyota Hilux whenever he wanted, and they could cruise around town and go wherever they wanted, including through the coveted drive-through.

When they got to the Hazard Zone, both boys were disappointed to see that it was closed.

"What kind of nightclub is closed on a Friday night?" Bradley said, kicking an empty can along the pavement. "That's bullshit."

"Too foul out," said the sausage sizzle man who was as usual set up outside the door to the club. Fridays were normally a roaring trade for him—bouncers would send would-be punters his way for a sausage to soak up some of the night's pre-drinks before letting them in the door. In exchange, they got free sausage sizzles and cans of Spree.

Tonight it was just him on the street.

"You boys want a sausage sizzle?"

Bradley shook his head. He didn't want sausages. He wanted cans of rum and coke, and to meet hot girls, and to drive out to the Heads under the frozen moon.

He wanted something to do—something that would transform him into somebody special. Somebody important.

It didn't look like it was the night. The boys decided to head homeward. Hayden planned to crash at Bradley's mum's place up the top of Bank Street.

They were despondent as they walked up the hill, hoods pulled tight against the misting rain, kicking at litter as they passed it.

"This is the kind of night that Smiley Frank would be about on," Hayden said.

Bradley shivered. He didn't want to think about Smiley Frank right now.

"I haven't seen him for a while," he said.

"No-one has. They say the cops raided his house and found a bunch of kids locked up in his back shed."

"No way," Bradley said. "I don't think he even has a house."

Hayden gave a low whistle. "Then what the hell did they raid?"

Smiley Frank was a local oddball who could often be seen wandering the streets of Vinetown with his umbrella clasped in one hand and a torch in the other. He always had a wide smile plastered on his face and smelled faintly of over-ripe fruit.

Nobody really knew his story, but the rumour was that he was on a sex offender list and could be arrested if he got anywhere near a school. Selection bias backed up the story—the children of Vinetown could all swear on their hearts and hope to die that they had never seen Frank near a school.

"Who told you that, anyway?" Bradley asked.

"My brother. He saw him get arrested, bro."

"Ay. Where at?"

"He was trying to get into a primary school apparently. A bunch of teachers had to come out and step him out but he wouldn't fuck off, so they called the cops."

"Far."

On a whim they turned off the pavement and started walking up the train tracks. The railway ran mostly parallel to Bank Street but took its own path along back alleys and through grassy culverts and tunnels.

"We could do some tags," Hayden said. "I know a mean spot."

"Go on."

Bradley was aware that neither of them had brought a Sharpie, but taking a look at this new spot would while away a few minutes. He scrambled up the rocky embankment on the far side of the railway tracks after Hayden.

There was a tall chain-link fence at the top of the rise.

"Are we going over this?" Bradley said. "I don't know, ay."

There was a single coil of barbed wire looped along the top of the fence. It was certainly surmountable—at least by anyone prepared enough to lay a heavy rug down over the top of it - but all the same, Bradley's memory of the last time he'd come home with his jeans all torn up was still fresh in his mind.

"Nah, I got a way," Hayden said. They made their way north along the fence, holding onto it to prevent themselves from falling back down the rise. Gravel gave way under their feet, setting off miniature avalanches down onto the train tracks.

"Any trains run at night?" Bradley asked.

"I don't know," said Hayden. He'd his hood off his head and was squinting up the railway line. "Who the fuck is that?"

"Huh?" Bradley followed his gaze. A figure loomed on the road bridge that crossed over the train tracks up ahead.

There were no streetlights in the area, but they could just make out his shape by the light of the moon. His silhouette was tall and thin, but with a round and bulbous circle where his head should have been.

Bradley was reminded of the proportions of a stick figure, the kind he would draw amongst the gridded squares of his maths book rather than figuring out what a and b and x were supposed to mean.

The man was still.

"Can he see us?" Bradley whispered over to Hayden.

"I don't think so. But that's where we're going, so he probably will once we get over there."

Bradley held out a hand to stop Hayden from continuing. "Wait. Look."

The man had begun to move. Without breaking his stare in what the boys presumed was their direction, the already tall-seeming figure grew taller, unfolding like a praying mantis. What had already been a stature pushing lankiness to its limits was actually a man kneeling on the pavement.

As he splayed his limbs out to walk away, it was like somebody had taken each extremity of the stick figure and pulled it out like spent chewing gum. He strode down the street and out of sight on stilt-like legs, his arms moving to his sides with their ends brushing his knees.

"Did you see that?" Hayden asked, a note of panic breaking his attempt at a whisper through into the audible.

"Shhh!" Bradley silenced him, almost as loudly. "What the fuck…"

They stayed huddled on the top of the gravel slope for a few more minutes, unable to tear their eyes away from the rail bridge. The rain had picked up again, and

Bradley could feel his hoodie start to get heavy and chilly against his skin.

"We've got to go," he said to Hayden. "Come on."

"Do you think it's gone?" Hayden said. He was a good six months older than Bradley, and the latter always looked up to him like an older brother. But suddenly Hayden sounded like a little boy again. The same kid who had cried when they watched *Jurassic Park* on video as kids.

But it remained a valid question. Bradley was still trying to tell himself that what he'd seen had just been some trick of the light or lack thereof—but another part of him couldn't help but imagine that figure walking through the empty streets in the rain, its bobblehead reaching the tops of buildings and able to step over parked cars.

"I didn't see anything," Bradley lied. "Let's go."

They got down on their asses and wriggled their way down the slope, passed caring about muddy jeans and wet shoes.

"Are you for real?" Hayden said. "I know you saw what I saw."

"I don't think you saw anything either," Bradley said. "It was dark *as* back there."

They crossed the train tracks and came through an alley into the streetlights of Bank Street. Bradley looked up and down the street and was relieved to see there was nobody around. Not even anyone of human proportions.

"That's bull, Bradley," Hayden said. "I know what I saw."

"You're fucking crazy, bro," Bradley said.

Hayden gave him a sharp shove in the chest that took the wind out of his lungs.

"Watch it," he said. His tone had lost almost all inflection—this was a serious warning.

The pair made their way up the long hill of Bank Street in silence. Bradley could feel the rain soaking through to his socks now. He was no longer keen on finding some booze or something exciting to do. Now he just wanted to get home.

They passed the dark and shuttered KFC. The McDonalds on the other side of the road still had a few cars passing through the drive-through.

"Maybe we can get a ride," Hayden said.

"No-ones giving us a ride, numb nuts."

Hayden shot Bradley a sharp look, but he'd already kept walking on up the hill.

His mum's place was up in the Regent, at the top of the hill. To get there he normally crossed through Regent Park, where there was a muddy bush track that took you right through the park without having to make the long trek around the block.

When they reached the gates to the park, Hayden was dawdling behind.

"I don't know," he told his friend. "Are you sure you want to go this way?"

Emboldened by a good twenty minutes of telling himself he'd seen nothing out of the ordinary, Bradley's fear had been all but extinguished. He'd rather cross through the park than spend the extra fifteen minutes plodding the wet pavement alongside his friend who he sometimes kind of hated.

"What, are you scared?"

"Fuck you, bro. I told you to watch it," Hayden said.

"Or what?"

"Or I'll fucking deck you, that's what."

Hayden had a good few inches on Bradley and tended to win every arm wrestle. A part of Bradley recognised that he was poking a sleeping bear that he didn't have the tools to deal with. But a louder voice in his mind was egging him on.

"As if," he said. "I'm not exactly afraid of a pussy who can't even walk through the park because he's scared of the dark."

He forged on ahead without waiting for Hayden's response, leaping up the slippery wet concrete steps that led to the bush track.

Suddenly, he was on his knees, his hands scraping against the steps and a hot pain blooming on the back of his head.

Hayden had punched him from behind.

"What the fuck, man!" Bradley yelled, spinning onto his back to face Hayden. The bigger boy was looming over him, so he scrabbled up onto the next step and got to his feet.

He ran down the path, being as careful as he could not to slip on the wet concrete without sacrificing speed. The path soon turned to mud. Potholes and puddles studded it in the dark. Bradley put a foot deep into a malleable space in the path at speed and found his centre of gravity careening out ahead of him.

"Ah, fuck," he grunted as he hit the ground. His hands had swung around behind him to cushion his landing, and both were immediately up to the wrists in the gritty clay.

Hayden was advancing on him. He stopped, maybe because he saw that his friend had taken a tumble.

"That's what you get, you prick," he said. He picked up a handful of mud and threw it at Bradley. "I warned you."

Bradley sneered at him in the dark and tried to wipe some mud from his face. His caked fingers just left more on.

Suddenly, a noise broke through the movement of trees in the wind. It was a loud creaking sound, like somebody had taken a wooden rowboat and stretched it to its furthest extreme. It was a sound that suggested a louder snapping sound was on the way.

"What the hell is that?" said Bradley, trying to get back to his feet.

Then the trees moved. Or more accurately, one of what they had both taken for a tree moved. It was a few metres up the path, an oddly straight sentinel that could have been a rimu or some other pine, until it split into two long legs and started stalking off through the trees.

There was a faint foul smell on the air, like rotting meat, or fruit left at the bottom of a school bag for the entire summer.

"It was that fucking thing again!" Hayden shouted. "We need to get the hell out of here!"

He grabbed Bradley by the hand and pulled him to his feet. They started back the way they had come, but as they turned they saw that the creature—or maybe another creature entirely with the same too slim proportions and dark silhouette— was blocking the path.

It looked like a tree had grown up over the track in the few moments it had been to the back of them.

"Forwards," said Bradley, pulling Hayden along with him. They scrambled down through the bush, slipping and sliding in the mud. At first Bradley thought it was just in his head, but soon he realised he could hear the noise again: that creaking sound, like an inorganic material screaming out in pain in the ultimate stress-test.

It made him think of the sander his dad had in the garage, or the high-pitched assault of an angle grinder.

It didn't just sound like it was behind them. It sounded like it was ahead, and to the left, and to the right. It was a surround-sound barrage of noise, and it was only getting louder.

"We've got to get over the bridge," Bradley said. The bridge marked the end of the bush track— it crossed a humble stream that made its way hear through the bullrushes and down a series of culverts to the harbour, where it joined the mangroves.

On the other side of the bridge were streetlights and parked cars and lit-up windows with people within who were having Friday night drinks or staying up to watch some late-night TV.

They thumped onto the bridge at full sprint, but this time it was Hayden's turn to tumble. His shoes hit the slippery wooden planks of the bridge and kept going, sending him hard down onto his ass.

"Come on!" Bradley shouted, turning to offer his friend his hand. In the few moments since they'd been at each other's throats, he'd managed to forgive everything. He'd think of that moment later to remind himself of just how easily he got a grip on forgiveness there in the dark.

But in that moment as he stopped to help his friend, he also became aware of that smell again— the rich, almost sweet bouquet of heat-caramelising flesh.

There was a shape beneath the bridge that wasn't supposed to be there. Unfolding out of the darkness was an arm that reminded Bradley of giant puppets he'd seen downtown one year. They'd been operated by multiple puppeteers, each using ropes to manipulate the giants' enormous papier-mâché limbs.

A huge grasping hand came into view first. It was maybe the size of a dust-bin lid—small in proportion to the creature's immense height. It was attached to an arm the shape and seemingly flexibility of a slender tree branch.

Then the head came out from under the bridge. Dark eyes looked up at them quizzically from underneath what looked like a huge motorcycle helmet. The top of its head was smooth and featureless, and apart from the eyes peering out through what look like glass, the rest of its features were obscured.

The creaking sound had become even more deafening. It rose in pitch until Bradley felt like it was coming from inside of his head. He felt his vision swim as the thing swung itself out from under the bridge and loomed over them.

Suddenly, a bright light shone on the creature. For just a moment, Bradley got a look at its features through the obscuring panel of dark glass covering its face. Apart from its huge dark eyes, it looked mostly human—a long narrow nose leading down to a mouth that was now open in what looked like a silent scream.

Apart from the smell, that's what stuck with him the most, when he couldn't sleep for years later and would sit up looking out into his backyard, second-guessing the stillness of every tree. It would have been better if it had the face of some storybook troll or Martian. He could have told himself that that's what it was. But it didn't look like any of those. It looked like a normal Vinetown resident in a motorcycle helmet—stretched into an unrecognisable shape by some unknown hand.

"Ho, there!" A voice from the end of the bridge. Bradley turned and saw the source of the light. A figure of more normal proportion was standing under an umbrella, with a torch focused on the creature above the boys.

"On your way, boy!" The figure shouted at it in a gruff voice.

The creature made another noise—a kind of defeated mewling. It brought its hands up to its face to block the light, meaning its elbows were stuck out at right angles like immense skeletal wings.

"Fuck off!" The man yelled at it, and it seemed to be complying. Bradley watched in wonder as it slunk back in jerky movements into the bush.

Then the man was with them, pulling them to their feet and mumbling under his breath.

"Those boys are always causing such a bloody ruckus," he said as they climbed the final stairway up to the street above. "Sorry about that."

Once they were in the streetlights they recognised their saviour. Smiley Frank was dressed in his usual worn-out windbreaker, with his umbrella above his head, his torch at his side and a rictus-like smile on his face. There was a faint smell clinging to him—so sweet it was almost sour, a kind of cloyed decay that hung around him like a cologne.

"Best get you boys home," he said. "Can't be out and about on a night like this."

They were all too happy to leave him standing there in the dark grinning to himself.

"And stay in the streetlights in future, huh boys?" He called out after them.

They had to sneak through Bradley's bedroom window, lifting it quietly to avoid Bradley's mum. It made no difference—her sharp ears heard them from the lounge, where she was up checking her watch and flicking listlessly through the channels.

She came through and berated Bradley for his muddy clothes and late return home and then told them to get ready for bed and to forget about playing any PlayStation that night.

By the time they'd showered and got ready for bed, both boys were yawning. The adrenaline had left their bodies, leaving them hollowed out.

They didn't talk about it that night.

And nor did they the next time Hayden slept over, which was also the last time. After that, he got snapped smoking weed at the back of the field and Bradley's mum soured on him. She forbade Bradley from hanging out with him, but that was hard to police when he was out wandering town.

They didn't talk about it through the years at parties where the rain bucketed down on bonfires and high school students fought for space on the barn floor to lay down and sleep.

They didn't talk about it as when they turned 18 and went inside the Hazard Zone for the first time to discover that it was an odd-smelling warehouse with sticky floors and unintelligible music.

They didn't talk about it when Bradley came home from uni in the holidays and saw Hayden at the Shoal Bay Tavern by chance. Hayden had proceeded to beat him atrociously at pool and make fun of his button-down shirt, but he made no mention of strange shapes in the forest, or that strange smell they'd both caught a whiff of at the odd moment through the years.

They didn't mention it years after that when Bradley walked past Hayden down by the river's edge. He nodded at his old friend in the single swift upwards motion that was expected at such encounters, but he didn't think Hayden saw him. Or maybe he just didn't recognise him.

Hayden had been pushing a stroller, his brow furrowed, and his eyes focused on the path in front of him.

Then one day he picked up the newspaper and found a little story buried near the back end. It had been syndicated down from the Vinetown Advocate.

Smiley Frank had died, and despite a long and lonely life of wandering, he now had dozens of community leaders and local business owners armed with stories about what a good guy he was.

Next to the story was a picture of him, dressed as he always was. Faded old blue rain jacket, red and white umbrella. The kind of torch boaties used for night fishing.

He'd walked himself into a heart attack.

Bradley skipped work and made the drive north, squinting through his windshield through torrents of rain. Up on the Brynderwyns he lost track of the road for a moment and felt like he was fording some raging river in an old Western.

The funeral wasn't well-attended, despite all the accolades in the paper. Bradley found a seat near the back and tried to see if there were any family members in the crowd. There was one old woman he thought bore a passing resemblance to Frank, but he wasn't sure.

His thoughts were interrupted by somebody sitting down next to him.

"How's it going, mate?" Hayden said. He was dressed in an ill-fitting black suit and smelled of aftershave. He had a backpack on which he took off and slid under the pew.

"Hey, mate," Bradley said. "Long time… sad, ay."

Hayden nodded soberly. "I've been thinking about stuff lately," he said.

"Yeah? What stuff?"

"You know." He nodded up towards the altar, where a large, framed photograph of Frank smiled back at them. "Frank. You. All of that."

Bradley nodded. He'd thought about it as well.

"See, the thing is… Frank was on his beat for what, 40 years?"

"What do you mean?" Bradley asked.

"Walking around town."

"Sure. I mean, my dad said he used to see him when he was a kid and everything."

"Exactly. And now he's gone." Hayden pulled out the backpack from under the pew and unzipped it. Bradley noticed people a few rows ahead were turning back and glaring at them.

Hayden had removed a torch from the backpack. It was one of those bright yellow ones with the wide beam. It was the same kind of torch that Frank had carried around Vinetown for decades.

"I'm taking the next shift," he said to Bradley. "But I wouldn't mind if you gave me a hand."

Someone from up ahead violently shushed, and Bradley nodded and focused his attention back on the altar. A priest was giving a sermon that seemed to have very little to do with Frank.

They played a slideshow after the sermon. Most of the photos were of Frank out and about, making his rounds. Umbrella slung over a shoulder and torch in hand. Many looked like they'd been taken from passing cars, derisively at the time and then later sent into the paper as some kind of tribute to the town character.

Bradley couldn't take his eyes off that same smile that appeared in every single picture of the man.

When the service was over, Bradley bummed a cigarette off Hayden in the carpark, and they smoked up against the side of the church to try and keep out of the rain.

"What do you say?" Hayden said. "I think someone's got to do it. That thing under the bridge… it touched us that night. I haven't really been able to get the smell out of my nostrils. I feel like it's been following me around all my life."

Bradley lifted his lit cigarette up into the air. "These kind of block it. A little bit. But I feel like it's time to quit." He remembered Hayden pushing the stroller down by the river. "You got kids now, right?"

"12 and 9," he said. "Soon they'll be the age we were."

Bradley took a deep puff and then coughed, suddenly reminded that he hadn't smoked a cigarette in years.
He thought about how next week was the shortest day of the year and how Vinetown's army of streetlights could only do so much.

He thought about how quickly the sun could drop up there in the so-called winterless north. How one moment you could be walking along the street on a brisk sunny day, and the next you were plunged into darkness.

He thought about himself, walking home from school on August evenings, rubbing at his arms to keep life in them, his feet baying from the cold from within their skins of wet cotton.

"You wouldn't happen to have another torch, would you?" He asked, motioning to Hayden's backpack. He'd need one if he was going to join his old friend on the beat. "Maybe we owe it to Frank to keep up his good work."

Hayden finished his cigarette and crushed it underfoot.

"Far, I knew you'd be keen," he said with a faint smile.

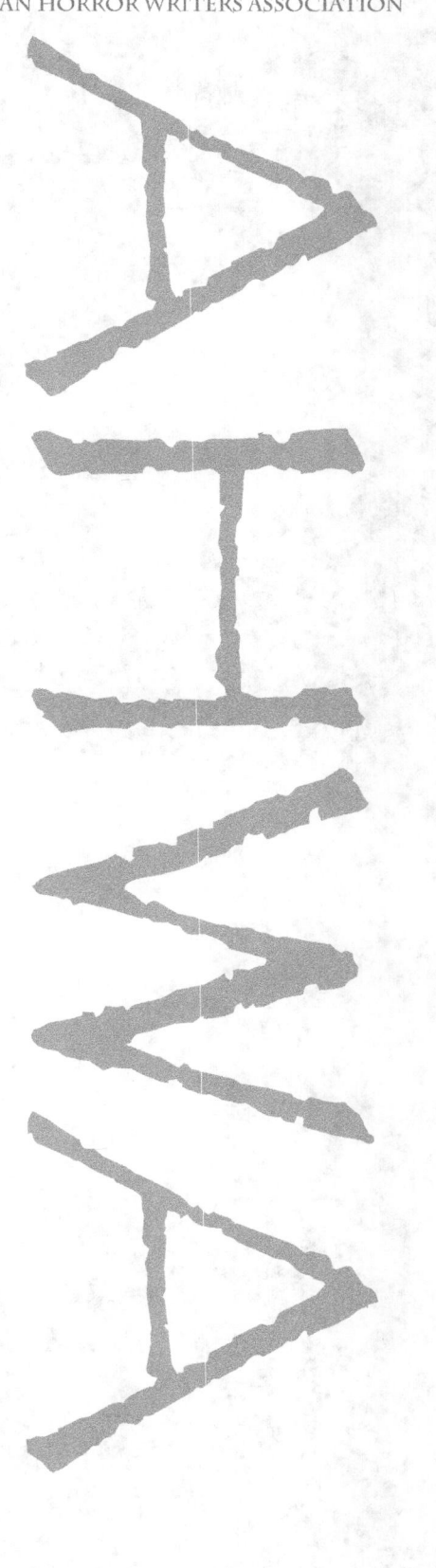

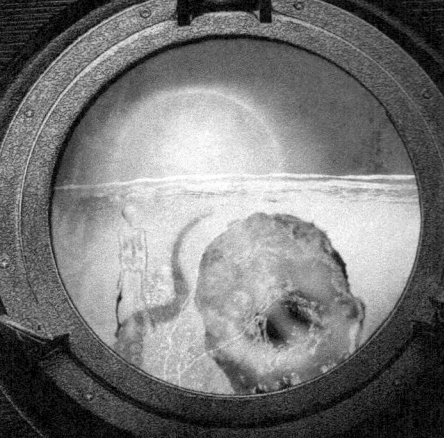

THE
AUSTRALIAN HORROR
WRITERS ASSOCIATION
PRESENTS

IN SUNSHINE BRIGHT
& DARKNESS DEEP
AN ANTHOLOGY OF AUSTRALIAN HORROR

ON SALE
NOW

HELL'S
BELLS

STORIES OF
FESTIVE FEAR
BY MEMBERS OF
THE AUSTRALIAN
HORROR WRITERS
ASSOCIATION

AHWA
australianhorror.com

## LEFT TO FESTER

# BY ZACHARY ASHFORD

Etienne had lived for a lot longer than he should have. Family legend said he should have died twenty years ago when he was first diagnosed with cancer, but since then, the irascible old bastard had trundled into so many of their funerals that Gabriel, his sister's son, was the only family member he hadn't outlived. With shaking hands gripping his walking stick and a grimace on his face, he'd inevitably hobble into the chapel to say goodbye to whichever of his nieces, nephews, cousins or friends had become the latest to beat him into a memorial urn, before spending his time there surveying the perimeter of the grounds for the one he called the Imposter.

Now, though, with a gun levelled on Gabriel, his hands were as calm as they'd been back in his days in the corps. Things had really gone to shit in the months that had passed since Gabe had knocked on his door and Etienne had grunted, led him to the kitchen table and shuffled around awkwardly.

"What did you want to tell me?" the boy had asked.

Today, Gabriel would be going nowhere, but things were different back then. "I need you to promise me something," Etienne had said.

"I won't die over there?"

"There's only you and me left, and someone else needs to know what I know, so shut up and listen."

Gabe had sighed. Rubbed his nose. "Fine. What is it?"

Etienne had begun his tale, desperate for Gabe to understand what was at stake.

***

"It happened after one of the big battles." The kettle whistled and Etienne, grateful for the chance to gather his thoughts, had got up to make coffee. "Those clever bastards really pinned us down. Shit, they probably would've wiped us out if the air-strike hadn't hit when it had. Not that it mattered to my friend Hank Cambridge. Before that first plane came in and lit up the forest, he took a rocket right to the chest. If there's one thing they can't train you for, it's watching someone who's saved your life a dozen times catch an explosive like a fucking medicine ball. When that happens and you taste that copper in the air, when you smell that barbecue, you either cope or you lose your mind. You remember that, because goddammit, there are times when you think something smells incredible. Then you realise the flames have found a dead body and you hate yourself a little more.

Etienne's mouth had felt dry. His hands trembled, like the old man he'd become. What he'd have given for a generous slug of bourbon to stop the shakes. But the story needed to be told. No more excuses.

"Cambridge had a family at home. Young baby. Wife. All that shit, and I couldn't bear to leave him there to rot like the rind of a goddamn T-bone. I was young like you. Naïve. The boss told us we'd return for the bodies, but I wasn't having it. His family, Deborah and the kid, they deserved better, so I went back there that night.

To be honest, I had no idea what I was going to find. You see bodies out there. They've been left in the sun and animals have gotten to them and there're parts that are congealing, oozing, rippling with maggots and insects, but somehow, in my head, I was still picturing Cambridge as this whole person. Clean and intact.

To this day, I still can't look in a butcher's window. Even in the moonlight, I could tell the rocket had done more than its work. The entire front of his chest was a mess. Intestines strewn everywhere, pulled apart by crows and God knows what else. His arms… they were minced and shredded like chuck beef. Shit, I spent ages looking for his head. Eventually, I realised the guys who bagged the bodies were right. I *couldn't* send him home. Poor Deborah would lose her mind. I owed her better.

Anyway, the whole missing-in-action thing, which is what I was, in effect, condemning Cambridge to, that's a steaming pile of horseshit. No one ever really goes missing in a ground war. Parts of them get blown to pulp, washed away in the rain, carried back to ant nests one morsel at a time and trodden underfoot, but people know where those men are; they know what happened to them. There's just an unspoken rule that says you don't send a person home to his grieving wife

when he's been parcelled into chunks like that.

And here's the thing, I'd thought that was bullshit for so long, but standing there, looking at how completely destroyed my friend was, I knew that there was no way he could be sent home. He would have to stay there. The way I came to see it, where he fell, something could grow.

Well, something did."

\*\*\*

Gabriel had fidgeted, certain Etienne had lost his mind. "What do you mean something did?"

Etienne had raised a hand to quiet him. Gabriel must have thought his uncle was a maudlin old fart opining an old tragedy, but it didn't matter. There was proof. "Are you going to listen?"

"Sorry. I just don't see—"

"I'm getting to it."

\*\*\*

"It bothered me for years; right up till the time I eventually decided the only way I could do something about that was to visit his family and tell them the truth. I looked them up in the phonebook after I came home. Their house was out in the country on a big block. Thing is, whenever I thought I finally had a good reason to go there and own up to my cowardice, I'd always invent a reason not to. And then the doctor told me I had cancer.

It was in the stomach. The same spot I always felt the guilt over Cambridge gnawing at me, funnily enough. Well, that gave me a good reason. If I didn't do it, I was going to take it all to the grave. I couldn't have that.

So I decided to go. Pay my respects.

When the door opened, my mouth dropped. The man at the door was

Cambridge. *The Cambridge.* The one I'd watched die. I'd seen his mutilated corpse and made the decision not to send him home in a body bag, but when he confronted me at that threshold, I knew I should have. I should have sent him home, because as much as whatever was pretending to be him looked like him, it wasn't him. It couldn't be. He was dead. Blown to pieces and picked apart by carrion eaters. What possible explanation could there have been for him to be back there in his own house?

***

"Are you sure you're remembering all this properly?"

Et wiped his mouth with the back of his hand. He'd never told it all before and he had to make sure he wasn't too harsh on the kid. It did sound implausible. "My mind's as sharp as it's always been."

Gabriel shifted uncomfortably in his chair. His coffee was still full. "Okay, what happened?"

***

"Cambridge didn't recognise me. Not exactly. If you asked me if there was some lingering sense of knowledge there, I would say maybe, but it wasn't a memory, that's for sure. Deborah had photos of us all. Cambridge used to send them to her. My guess is he'd seen those, but he still couldn't place me. I'd changed too by then. My hair was gone. I'd shrunk. Grown a beard. Withered.

Just as I was about to take my leave, Deborah came up behind him. Her recognition was a thing to behold! She called my name and hugged me tight. She told me I should have kept in touch and then she invited me in for dinner.

The imposter watched this unfold without saying too much of anything, but when it became clear I was supposed to be an old war buddy of his, he gave me a big hug too. You ask me, the bastard just played along. I'll tell you now, though, there was a frostiness there that I don't think Deborah noticed.

Although, to be truthful, if she had have noticed anything, I think she still might have left us sitting there on opposite sides of a table with a six-pack of beers, a chess-set and a nasty truth between us. As you can probably imagine, I was looking for scars on this guy. Signs of shrapnel-wounds. Signs that—despite the unholy impossibility of it— he'd somehow regenerated from the scattered meat he'd been when I saw him last. In my head, I knew I should be discrete, but let's face it, I probably wasn't.

He watched me closely too. Of course, I say 'he'. What I should be saying is 'it'. As the night went on and our games of chess fell into a pattern, I noticed some strange things about this so-called Cambridge. Now, we all know that war can do things to a man. It can break him and it can change him, but not one of my old war buddies ever had their fundamental behaviours changed. I knew Cambridge, and during a game of chess, that cheating son of a bitch always licked his lips and squinted while he was thinking. We used to give him hell for it. This thing didn't do that. It was completely passive. You ever heard the saying 'still waters run deep'? Well, still waters were the very definition of Cambridge's chess-face now. And if there was one thing that, in life, he never was, that one thing was calm. The man had ants in his pants.

After some time, I decided to spit it out. 'I

don't know who you are,' I said. 'But you're not Cambridge. Cambridge is dead.'

He looked at me like he'd trodden in dog shit and I was the inconvenience on the bottom of his shoe.

'Is that so?' he asked.

He began to tap one of the chess pieces— a bishop if I remember correctly— on the table and he asked me again. 'Is that so?' Then his lip started to twitch. You ever seen a death adder wriggle its tail so it can trick other predators into coming too close? Well, picture his lip moving like that.

'Makes you wonder why you'd want to visit a dead man's wife. Makes you wonder why all these years have passed and you haven't said jack shit. Makes you wonder what benefit there is in telling anyone the truth,' he said.

And then, for just a moment, his face changed. That twitching in his lip moved across his cheeks and beneath his skin and it revealed the truth to me like a nightmare unfurling from the fires of hell. That face was like a melting pile of eyes and mouths, tongues and assholes atop a chasm of teeth.

If I'd have blinked, I'd have missed it, but I didn't. I saw it and somewhere real deep in the reptilian fibre of my brain stem, a sense of panic like I'd never felt before set in.

'What are you?' I asked it.

And that was when I finally saw some passion in its eyes. Some spark of life.

'I'm what happens when you leave things behind and let them fester,' it said. 'I'm the darkness that grows out of hasty decisions. I'm the thing that eats you from the inside.' With that, he placed the bishop on the board. 'Your move.'

\*\*\*

Gabriel had checked his watch at that point of the story, no doubt thinking it was time to call the men in white coats. Pinned by misplaced guilt, though, he'd sat there with the wide eyes of a child. "So what did you do?"

"I made my excuses and left."

"You left? That's it?"

"No, that's not it, but you have to wait a second. I gotta empty this goddamn bag." He prodded the colostomy bag. "Unless you wanna help me with that."

"You're on your own."

Etienne came back a few moments later, this time putting two beers on the table, cracking them with the lip of one of the chairs.

\*\*\*

"I didn't tell you the worst part about me leaving that night. The bastard laughed me out of the door. Even as I said my goodbyes to Deborah, he stood beside her, laughing his ass off. But, like I told you before, that first visit sure as shit wasn't the end of it. First of all, you've gotta remember that my original goal was telling Deborah that Hank was dead. Not only had I completely failed in that, I'd been shocked into taking it all tacitly. I could console myself by saying I'd challenged him, but when I thought about that game of chess, I wasn't sure how I didn't piss my pants.

I'd thought I'd learned the meaning of fear during the war. I thought about fear a lot after that encounter with Cambridge, or as I began to think of him, the Imposter. Turns out in the war, I was scared, but it was a life and death thing. A mortal thing. The way I felt when that thing, *the Imposter*, revealed itself to me was something different. It was a gnawing anxiety that I still feel today. You've seen how my hands shake. They never did before I saw that thing. Anyway, the fallout of this was that I forced myself to harden the fuck up and get back to the mission.

Could that thing hurt me or kill me? I supposed it could, but so what? I was an old man with cancer and I'd faced down situations that could kill me before. If it did, it did, but I decided I needed to be smarter and focus on my goal. To tell Deborah that I had chosen to let Hank rot rather than send him home to be buried.

I tracked her down at work and convinced her to have lunch with me. You know what she asked? 'Are you coming back to see Hank again soon?' Like hell, I was. Not that I told her that.

'That's actually what I came here to talk about,' I said.

Now, this whole time my mind was screaming at me to slow it down and to break it to her easily, but the hairs on my arms were standing on end and my balls had climbed so far inside my gut, I thought I was going to have a heart attack. I had to spit it out.

'Hank, your Hank—he's dead. I watched him die. He was MIA because he took a rocket to the chest. There was nothing left of him. I couldn't find his head, Deborah. I looked and I looked and I looked, but I couldn't find it, and the army, it has this policy not to send home corpses that could have a traumatic effect on families.' It wasn't only my hands shaking, that much I can truly say. 'I meant to save you pain and agony, Deborah. I'm sorry.'

She sorta stopped chewing and she dabbed at her lips with her napkin. 'But Hank's at home, Et,' she said. 'You know

that.'

I was crying like a little bitch by this stage and I shook my head and I clenched my fists so she wouldn't see my hands shaking. 'I don't know how long he showed up after the rest of us got back home, but that's not him,' I said. 'That thing that looks like Hank is something else. That's an imposter. I know it is because he didn't know who I was. Not really, and I think you kinda picked up on that, but when I challenged him, he revealed himself and I don't know what he wants, but it's not good, Deborah. It's not good.'

Her lips pursed and her eyes hardened and then she spoke. 'I don't know who you think you are, Etienne, but if you think you can take my happiness away after all these years, you can go right back to wherever you came from.'

That bitch had known all along.

'Do you think I can't tell the difference between the Hank that came back and the man I loved—the father of my children?' she said. Her shoulders went up and down like the tide, but she wasn't sad. She was seething. You could hear it in the little gusts of wind she blew out of her pinched nose. 'But while that might not be my Hank, he's the Hank that his baby son knows and he came back to us.' She laid money out on the table and stood up. 'Do you know what he asks of us, Et?'

I shook my head.

'Exactly. You don't know anything, so take your guilty conscience and stay away from us. I don't want to see you again. Do whatever it is you have to do to forget Hank and move on, but stay away from us.'

With that, she walked off. For the most part, I did what she said. I could even say I'd forgotten it all if it weren't for one thing.

***

Etienne had looked into Gabe's stupefied face and raised a finger when the boy made to speak. From his pocket, he pulled a crumpled piece of paper, smoothed it out on the table and thrust it in front of his nephew.

"What's this?"

"Read it. Then ask questions."

Gabriel reached for it. "Are you sure?"

Etienne nodded. "Read it aloud, he'd said."

And so Gabriel did.

*Dearest Etienne,*

*By this stage, your long illnesses must surely have become as burdensome as the guilt you carry. Rest assured, this earthly torment will be over soon. Only one remains for you to farewell and he's off to war. You could probably pick him off yourself if you were inclined to hasten your passage out of this world, but let's be honest, the war will more than likely do it for him. From there it's all pitchforks, brimstone and the butcher's block for you.*

*Yours,*

*Hank Cambridge.*

When Gabe had finished reading, Etienne nodded. "And now you know why I called you here. I meant it before. I need you to promise me something."

***

All of that had been before Gabe went to war and it had led to this moment in the here and now. This time, they settled in Et's living room, close to the warmth of the fire. Gabe leaned back on the low sofa while Etienne sat forward on his recliner, holding the freshly oiled revolver with a steady hand. "Your promise, Gabe?"

His nephew shifted on the couch, firmly within sight of the gun's black and empty eye. "Is that why you asked me to come here?"

"I want to know that you kept it. That you didn't leave anyone behind. That you didn't make my mistake."

"Things are different now, Uncle. No one was left behind."

"No one?"

"No one."

"I've been following everything pretty closely in the papers and I know about the Battle of the Burned. The fire in that refinery."

Gabriel's eyes narrowed. "Somehow, we all made it out. That was…a hectic night. I thought I was done for."

"But you weren't."

"I'm here."

"And no one was left behind?"

"No one."

Etienne thrust the gun forward, as if prodding some unseen person. "I've seen action, Gabe. I know what it's like. People die in those battles. People get trapped and caught in crossfire and left behind. You think I'm just a crazy old man. You think I'm living in some fantasy-land made of guilt and bitterness, and that my story can't possibly be true, but I know, Gabe. I know it's true."

"You know it's true?"

"Hank the impostor. The battle. All of it. Truer than the sky is blue." Etienne blasted a shot into the brick fireplace. Centred the gun back on his nephew's torso. Cool smoke ghosted into the air.

***

"I saw him again, Gabe. I couldn't let it slide. That letter played on my mind something fierce. Wouldn't let me sleep. Wouldn't let me breathe. All I could think about was the fact that so many had died prematurely while I lived on, completely ready for death. Shit, there were times I almost hoped you would die over there. At least that way, I could be sure my time was finally coming. Lord knows I'm sick to death of this fucking place. And then I read about the Battle of the Burned, and the pain in my gut, the cancer that had been dormant for so long, came back with a vengeance. I thought I was apt to keel over and die that day, and I realised if the bastard tumour that was supposed to kill me so long ago had decided to flare up again then, well, I think you know what I'm saying.

To be certain, I went back to Hank and Deborah's. This time, when I got to the door, Hank was waiting. You should've seen the smile on his face as he gestured me inside and tried to direct me to the basement. Beneath his grin, his real face was there like a foot in an ill-fitting sock. I don't know why it was so much harder for him to hide it this time. Perhaps he felt he didn't need to, but nevertheless, it was obvious that something completely inhuman shifted beneath the skin.

'No basement,' I told him, so we stopped in the lounge-room where Deb sat reading. She hadn't aged at all, Gabe. Not one bit. I can't explain that, but whatever had taken Hank's place was capricious. While it had clearly been playing games with me, it was capable of love. That much was obvious in the serenity of Deborah's face. She was youthful and happy and as corrupt as the devil himself. 'You're going to stay away from my nephew,' I said.

He laughed. He actually laughed. 'That one dies because of his own decisions. If he hasn't already.' He pointed at the dining table in the corner of the room and gestured for me to sit. 'You'll never know if he returns or if *something that grows* in the spot where he bleeds out takes his place.' He was fiddling around with a decanter on the cabinet by this point. Pouring glasses of brandy. 'You really should have taken the advice I gave you in the letter, and killed him yourself before he left. It would have saved you a lot of hassle.'

I didn't even tell him to shut up. I'm old and I've lived longer than I ever should have. I took the gun from my belt and I blew him away. One, two, three pulls of the trigger and he went reeling backwards and crashed to the ground. There was a commotion behind me. Deborah was out of her seat, standing with her mouth agape. She started to age right before me. Her hair thinned. Her skin creased. Her spine curved. For me, that settled it. She was just as culpable. I put one right through her forehead, spinning her like a ballet dancer.

And that's when I heard the bubbling sound. Cambridge was changing too. The face I knew was melting away and the real one that he kept beneath the mask was seeping into view. Deb bled like any normal person who'd been shot in the head, but Hank, he was slowly oozing away into something else. Like I said, whatever it was that came back all those years ago wasn't Hank. It was an imposter.

My business done, I set a match to the curtains and let the fire consume the evidence.

***

Etienne steadied his hand around the revolver. "Naturally, I had a lot of time to let the implications of everything play out before you returned." With the other hand he pulled another crumpled letter from his dressing gown and flicked it at Gabriel's feet. "And then that arrived."

Gabe shook his head. "I know what that is, Et. It's an MIA letter and I can explain."

"So can I."

"No, you can't. I should have contacted you, but I couldn't risk it." Slowly, as if careful not to stun his uncle into action, he picked the letter up. "The date coincides with that battle you mentioned. The Battle of the Burned. That's because I knew I had to get away. We set that fire. The soldiers on our side over there, they've gone crazy. They're just butchering everyone. That fire wasn't a pitched battle. It was a massacre, committed so we could take the oil. They weren't even soldiers we were killing."

"Bullshit. We wouldn't do that."

"You know we do that. I had to leave, Et. I went AWOL."

Etienne cocked the hammer. The dull ache in his stomach throbbed. Shifted. "Prove it to me, Gabe. Prove that you're really you."

"Your story, Et. If it's true like you say it is, then shouldn't you be dead? If your curse was to outlive us all…to wallow in that misery—

"What, you think I'm going to just drop? Keel over like a wind-up toy that's out of juice?" He snorted. "I don't think so, but I suppose we'll find out in a minute."

"You're making a mistake."

The old man appeared to mull it over. "I don't think that story of yours makes any sense, Gabe. I don't think you're gonna get a letter sent home because you went AWOL. There'd have been MPs here. Contact."

"There were so many bodies. That's what made it the perfect time to go. Without pulling the teeth out of every corpse before they threw it in a mass grave, they could never be certain."

Etienne fired.

Gabriel's body rocked as the bullet drove him backwards.

Something squeezed the tumour in Etienne's stomach. Twisted. He fell to his knees at the base of the recliner then crawled to his nephew's prone body. His head was ringing from the sound of the gunshot, but any second now, he'd hear that bubbling sound Hank had made. He had to. In the distance, he heard a siren, but not the melting noises he expected. He pulled himself to a squat. The pain in his stomach almost tearing him apart.

There, what he saw on the couch was almost enough to send his mind on holiday. The brains and gore on the headrest and curtains behind it were one thing, but the front of Gabe's head was, aside from the bullet-wound in his temple, perfectly normal.

Et had to deal. He had to hold onto what was happening and lock it into his mind as real and not something he'd imagined. Had to cope with the mistake or lose his mind.

The siren blew up louder and blue and red lights flashed in the driveway. There were footsteps outside. In Etienne's mind, an idea was growing. Hank hadn't been real. He'd been a personification of the guilt he'd felt. Had been post-traumatic stress. Had been a symptom of his madness.

There were three loud knocks at the door. "Police! Open up!"

Etienne inspected Gabe's corpse one last time, desperate for some sign his nephew had lied about the battle, had been an imposter. He saw none. Only a boy he'd loved, who'd trusted him, now dead.

The officer knocked again. Louder.

Etienne reached for the gun, rested it against his temple. Closed his eyes. He hadn't keeled over when he'd murdered Gabe, but perhaps he could speed things along. He had, after all, lived for a lot longer than he should have.

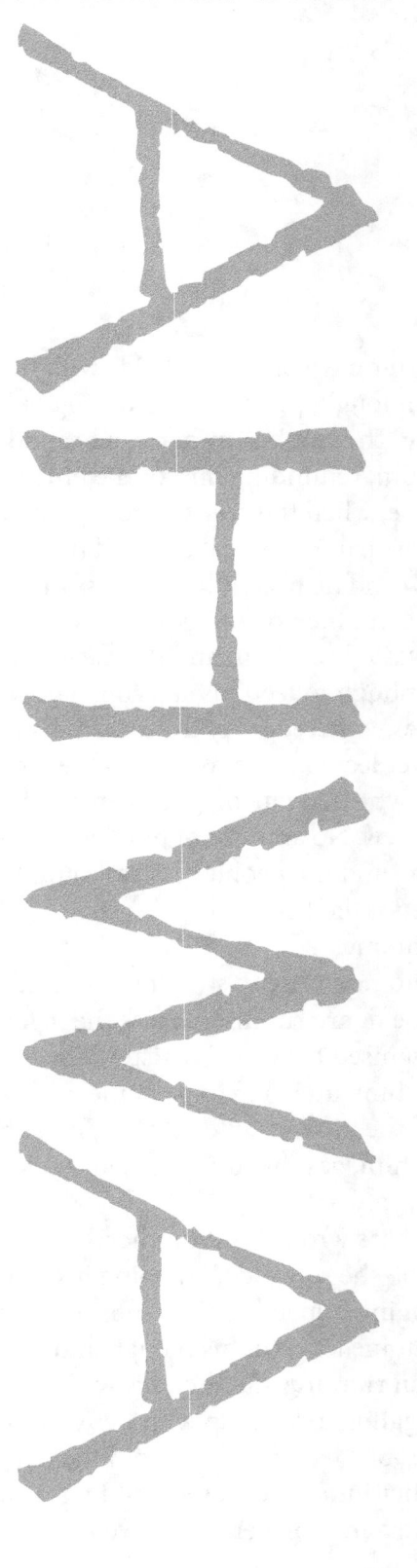

# THE DANCING PLAGUE

## BY A.M. JOSEPH

Antoine worked the fields with his plough, pulled by a grunting old pony. The harsh summer sun beat down on him, reminding him of the bitter year before, when the crops were dry and dead for the harvest. Sweat dripped from his brow and he tasted the saltiness on his lips. Antoine hoped his work would not be wasted yet again and the harvest would be enough to feed his starving family. His father withered away from sickness last winter leaving him to tend to the farm on his own—the fate of many other families he knew. No amount of praying could save them, and the people of Strasbourg had called it the Bad Year.

"Antoine!"

Antoine stood up straighter, squinting at a lone figure running across the field. He recognised his younger sister, Adrienne, bunching up her skirt as her legs leaped over the mounds of dirt. She almost fell into him, gasping for breath and struggling to form words.

"What's wrong? Is it mother?"

"No," she squealed, grabbing his arm, and dragging him away. "You must come see!"

Antoine let go of his plough and began running after her, his weary body struggling to keep up with her vibrant steps. She led him away from the fields and further into the city, the buildings getting thicker and thicker as they ventured through the maze of streets. They emerged into the marketplace where farmers were selling this season's harvest, the craftsmen and artisans selling all manner of goods which their family could not afford. An old cobbler toiled at a pair of leather shoes at his stall, several identical pairs piled up behind him. He raised his head as the two siblings passed him.

There was a small crowd gathering, though they were not interested in the leather, or the tools, or the woven cloth, or the trinkets. The people were staring at something, and Adrienne began to point her finger eagerly. Antoine followed her line of sight, peering over the shoulders of the small group to see a lone woman dancing, only there was no music and no smile on her face. Some people cheered her on but there was an unsettling silence in the square as everyone watched her feet step across the cobbles. He recognised the woman as Frau Trauffea and the crowd murmured as she danced, skipped, leapt, spun.

"She's been here since the morning," someone said. It was already mid-afternoon.

"I'll fetch Brother Thomas," said Antoine to no one in particular, then he pulled Adrienne aside. "You are not to come back here."

She frowned at him but obeyed, skipping

her way down the streets in the direction of the farm. Antoine went in the opposite direction, towards the cathedral.

The city of Strasbourg was well known for its clergyman. Brother Thomas had tended to the funeral of Antoine's father and the holy man understood the ways of inexplainable things. He was always in the cathedral at the centre of the city. The doors often remained locked when the clergymen were gathered inside. Brother Thomas had said they were praying for the people of Strasbourg, whose sins had caused the Bad Year, the dying crops, the starvation, and the death.

Antoine beat on the oak doors of the cathedral. A plump man with a balding head peered through the small crack, glancing up and down before recognising the young boy.

"Antoine!" he beamed, though the door did not open any wider.

"Brother Thomas, something strange is happening in the square."

"There is always something strange happening in the square." The clergyman chuckled, a clamour of voices and clinking sounds behind him.

"It's Frau Trauffea. She dances is the streets where no music plays."

"Then strike up a tune," he laughed. "What harm can one woman do?"

"But…"

The door slammed shut, more laughter and voices resounding from inside the church.

*** 

The next day, Adrienne watched as Frau Trauffea danced through the streets. Other people had joined her, and they had danced all day and all night. She admired their dedication. Adrienne had always wanted to dance. She had heard of the great theatres in Paris where performers with fancy costumes had the skill to leap through the air and spin on their toes, their gaze fixed to an adoring crowd.

Instead, she was stuck on the farm, with tousled hair, grimy hands, and a torn dress. Mud covered her from head to toe and no matter how much she bathed, she could not be rid of it. Adrienne watched Frau Trauffea, a young woman with a grace and beauty which she could never possess. She wanted to join her under her dancing spell, with not a care in the world.

Then something strange began to happen. Frau Trauffea's movements became more frantic, her head lolled left and right, and her legs kicked out in strange directions. It was like she was being mangled, an invisible force pulling her in every direction.

Then the screaming started.

Frau Trauffea cried and shouted as her movements became even more erratic. The crowd parted with murmurs of alarm as she twisted and shook around the marketplace. It was then that Adrienne noticed the blood on her feet.

The other dancers began to scream with her, a deafening sound. Adrienne covered her ears with her hands and stumbled backwards.

Frau Trauffea's body quivered and her eyes rolled to the back of her head as if she was possessed. The exhausted woman finally collapsed to the ground, but the damage she caused could not be reversed. Throngs of women and men were already dancing through the streets shaking and shouting like their bodies were lit on fire, screaming, and pleading with the bystanders to help them.

Adrienne backed away as a group of people rushed over to lift Frau from the ground. The crowd began to swallow her up, then someone seized her from behind. She let out a squeal.

"What are you doing here?" Antoine spun her around, his grip biting into her shoulders. "I told you to stay away from here!"

"It's only dancing…"

"No, Adrienne. Go home to mother."

"You can't tell me what to do. You're not father!"

"But I can beat you just as good as him." Adrienne pressed her lips together, a pout forming. Antoine sighed then patted her on the shoulder. "Just go help mother, Adrienne. She needs you."

Adrienne nodded then turned her back to him, hiding her expression of distaste. She did not like fighting with Antoine, but he was always telling her what to do. Her feet stamped along the cobbles as she headed in the direction of home.

*** 

A few days later, Antoine returned to the marketplace to collect supplies. His eyes widened when he saw that the number of people dancing had more than doubled since his last visit. At the centre, dozens of people gathered to dance and dozens more gathered to watch them, surrounding them in a circle as if they were entertainers from a foreign country. A once in a lifetime spectacle. Antoine squeezed amongst the murmuring crowd to get a better look.

"It must be the warm weather," said one.

"I think it is the devil's work," said another.

"Saint Vitus has cursed them for being sinners," agreed the man beside him. "A woman started all of this. Women are the devil's gateway."

A man crumpled to the ground and joined the others who had collapsed from their dancing fit, lying unmoving as the other dancers continued around them, sometimes trampling their bodies, before they were taken way. No one knew where to. Only that the city council and clergymen had arranged for them to receive healing. The physicians in the neighbouring cities had been sent for and were to arrive this afternoon. A meeting would be held in the cathedral and Antoine wanted to listen.

When he was a child, Antoine was friends with one of the altar boys. He would let him inside the sacristy at the back of the church to show him the fine robes, hangings and linens that adorned the cathedral and to talk with him about God. There was a window with a broken latch which Antoine could climb through whenever he wanted, but he stopped visiting when his father started making him work on the farm. He was only ten.

Now Antoine pulled open the wooden shutters and climbed through the window, a wave of nostalgia washing over him as he slid through. He toppled onto the floor almost knocking over the vestments hanging on a rack.

"The people are calling it the Saint Vitus Dance." Antoine recognised the resonant voice of Brother Thomas. The clergymen, magistrates and physicians had gathered in the church for their meeting, a wooden door the only thing separating the sacristy from the echoey room of the cathedral.

"They dance because their blood is hot," said an older man.

"What is your remedy?" Brother Thomas

spoke.

"You must let them dance."

The voices jumbled together as more than one man spoke, the sounds bouncing off the walls of the hollow hall. Antoine struggled to hear what they were saying.

"We'll hire musicians and dancers," said Brother Thomas. "The people will dance until they cannot dance anymore."

"And if that doesn't work?" asked another voice.

"Then God has passed His judgement on them…"

\*\*\*

Adrienne stirred the pot of stew over the fireplace, a brown liquid with only a handful of barley from their thin harvest and scraps of meat Antoine traded for at the marketplace. Its scent was faint and would do little to nourish them. She sat at the dining table while she waited for it to boil. Her mother sat opposite her, staring at the skirt she was mending with her needle and thread.

"Dinner will be ready soon," said Adrienne.

Her mother only nodded; her gaze fixed on her work. She barely spoke since her husband died and Adrienne often caught her staring into the distance for minutes, even hours on end. The wisps of grey hair and lines under her eyes had become more during the past year, and it was like she had gone forward in time, leaving Adrienne and Antoine behind. Now she was an old woman. An old, broken woman hollowed out by the Bad Year which had taken everything from her. Left her with a failing farm and fatherless children.

"They're going mad out there!" Antoine shut the front door behind him and dropped a sack of supplies on the table.

"What's happening?" Adrienne leaped up from her chair, then slowly slid down again when Antoine joined them at the table.

"They're hiring musicians to play in the marketplace… and dancers… to dance with them."

"Professional dancers? From Paris?"

"Yes. The physicians think that more dancing will cure them. People who have not become sick yet have joined the dance to help them heal faster." Antoine saw the gleam in his sister's eye, and he gave her a stern look. "Don't even think about going out there."

"But I want to see."

"You're not going anywhere near the marketplace or the city until this is over."

"I want to help too, Antoine. Some of our friends are out there!"

"There's nothing for you to worry about. Brother Thomas is doing all he can. He has God on his side."

Adrienne stood from the table and pressed her lips together as she served each of them a bowl of the stew. They ate in silence for a while, letting the tasteless liquid fill them, before Antoine spoke again.

"How about you help me on the farm tomorrow?" he said, slurping from his spoon. "I know father never let you but you're old enough now."

So Antoine and Adrienne avoided the marketplace for the next week, working together to do the chores on the farm. They rationed their food so they would not have to go into the city, though the music carried through the wind and Adrienne could not help but listen.

\*\*\*

Antoine opened his eyes, the dawn light

habitually waking him. He dressed himself and prepared for the day's work before he wandered to where Adrienne and his mother slept. The straw mattress that they shared was empty, his mother already awake and staring out the tiny window.

"Where is Adrienne?" he demanded. When his mother did not respond he grabbed her shoulders and shook her. "Mother! Where is Adrienne?"

The woman smiled, looking at him. "Her father calls to her."

Antoine released his mother and ran for the door, sprinting across the field towards the city.

Music sounded at the heart of Strasbourg as the people gathered in the marketplace. The merchants and churchgoers had removed the stalls under the direction of Brother Thomas, to make room for a large wooden platform. The musicians played their shrill strings, shimmering tambourines and beating drums as the people danced on and around the stage. The air reeked of sweating bodies and filth from the city streets.

The cobbler was the only one who remained in his corner of the marketplace, watching Antoine from where he sat. One by one, he dipped the leather shoes he had made into a dark, swirling dye. When he pulled them out, they dripped with a crimson red.

Antoine pushed his way through the thickening crowd, the music thumping in his ears. He had not returned to the marketplace for days, and the number of dancers had increased to more than a hundred. They tossed their limbs, ruffled their skirts, and flung their heads to the tempo while onlookers hollered and cheered them on to dance away the illness of the Saint Vitus Dance.

He finally emerged to the line of people in the front, angling his head upwards to watch the dancers on the stage. There were professional performers from Paris in their colourful garments with flowing ribbons, dancing alongside the crazed citizens of Strasbourg. Antoine's eyes scanned the group, widening when he saw the most unholy sight.

His sister Adrienne was among them spinning in circles, her head tilted to the heavens. Sweat dripped from her brow and her face twisted in anguish as the illness took her, keeping her under its sinful spell. The stamping feet vibrated through the wood and splashed him with hot blood, its metallic smell filling his nostrils. Antoine tasted it at the back of his throat as he shoved past the other dancers and scaled the steps to the platform. He seized his sister's shoulders.

"Stop this madness!" he screamed, his voice barely carrying over the noise.

For a moment Adrienne looked at him, a tear running down her cheek. "Help me, brother!"

Her dancing resumed with even more vigour as she threw herself around the stage wildly. She pushed Antoine away in one great movement and he fell over the edge of the platform into the crowd below.

***

Antoine ran as if a fire licked at his heels, all the way to the cathedral, beating once again on the closed door.

"Brother Thomas!" he cried, ramming his fists over and over again.

Finally, the door opened, a clergyman looking down on him with a grimace. Antoine pushed past him before he could protest and strode down the aisle of the church. The clergymen sat at a table, the altar, where a feast was laid out. Mouth-watering meats, sweet fruits and delectable cheeses piled high in their plates and pungent alcohol filling their goblets to the brim.

"What's all this?"

"My boy," Brother Thomas stood from his seat at the centre of the table.

"My sister is sick with the St Vitus dance. You must help her."

"We are doing all we can." Brother Thomas walked towards him, his arms outstretched.

Antoine dodged the embrace, his face twisted in revulsion. "The city is in madness, yet you sit here in your church and do… nothing. You let them dance to their deaths!"

"The sinners will be taken care of. You have nothing to fear."

"My sister is not a sinner. She is only a child…She is ill."

"This plague will be ended tonight."

"How? What are you going to do to them?"

"My boy," Brother Thomas smiled, his lips still dripping with red wine, but his eyes remained cold. "You needn't worry."

"If you will do nothing to help my sister then I will take her away from this city."

The smile vanished entirely from the holy man's face as Antoine turned to leave. One of the other clergymen barred the young boy's way out and Brother Thomas seized a laden silver tray from the table, swinging it at the back of his head. Antoine fell, grapes and loaves of bread scattering on the ground as he lay there unconscious. Two of the clergymen lifted his limp body and tossed him into the sacristy, bolting the door.

***

Music was banned in Strasbourg by order of the city magistrates. They sent away the Parisian dancers and musicians, the four hundred people remaining in the marketplace, twitching, shaking, convulsing to nothing. Only their cries pierced the eerie silence of the square as the rest of the citizens huddled in their homes. The cobbled paths and wooden stage were streaked with dry and fresh blood. People had collapsed from exhaustion, trampled by the feet of other victims as they groaned and laboured for breath. Foaming at the mouth, some rose up again to resume their deathly frenzy. Others did not get up at all, their bodies already rotting where they lay, foul odours poisoning the air. Thoughts swirled in Adrienne's head as her feet and body and mind would not obey her. She remembered Antoine who had not come back for hours. Or was it days?

A group of men, merchants, and church members entered the square. Brother Thomas and the other clergymen stood with them, pointing at the Saint Vitus dancers. One by one they were seized and dragged out of the marketplace. The dancers kicked their legs as they were strapped with bristly rope to wagons and wheeled away. Still, they tried to dance even as the men piled them on top of each other, packed them together like squirming, writhing fish. Adrienne screamed till her lungs were hoarse, her limbs convulsing hysterically.

The wagons rolled out of the city walls pulled by trotting horses, following each other in a line down the winding path to the shrine of Saint Vitus. The musty grotto lined with moss and overgrown foliage was where the people worshiped and brought their offerings to the saint. It was nestled amongst the hills above the nearby town of Saverne.

After a few hours of travelling, the trotting horses grinded to a halt. Brother Thomas and the other men took the feverish dancers inside the shrine, where a wooden figurine of Saint Vitus stood at the centre. They removed the dancers' worn shoes which clung to their bloodied feet and replaced them with new ones, dyed red. There were crates of them, newly made, in a corner of the grotto. Once they were fitted, a priest led the people in a circle around the statue and, as they continued to dance, the other clergymen threw holy water and shouted for Saint Vitus to free them of his curse. Adrienne quivered each time the drops landed on her exposed skin.

*** 

Antoine rode on the back of the old pony, following the trail to the shrine of Saint Vitus. There was a dull ache in his head, but he kept going, hoping he would find his sister there. He was glad for the curiosity of his youth, for he would not have known about the broken latch on the window in the sacristy. When he awoke, the corrupt clergymen had taken the dancers, the marketplace left empty and silent with nothing but the stained cobblestones revealing the chaos that had gone on before.

Antoine pulled at the reins, the hills looming before him and the entrance to the shrine only a small distance away. Dozens of wagons were abandoned outside, the horses and mules left tethered to them. He walked up the path and entered the grotto, voices echoing like

ghosts as he ventured deeper inside. He emerged into the small room where the wooden statue of Saint Vitus stood at the centre, water dripping from the ceiling. The dancers paraded around the statue still screaming as the brothers and priests threw holy water at them. None of them were his sister, so he scanned the room to the bodies lying in rows on the floor, the merchants and churchgoers adding to the mass of people as the hours passed.

Antoine sank to his knees as his eyes rested on his sister's body, cold and still. He buried his face in his hands and wept, tears flowing down his cheeks. Then a gentle hand rested on his shoulder, and the grief-stricken boy looked up. Brother Thomas smiled at him, but Antoine scrambled to his feet.

"Your sister is free from the curse," the older man said.

"She is not free," cried Antoine. "Your evil wiles have killed her!"

"I've saved her from her sins!" said Brother Thomas.

"She was not a sinner… she only wanted to help…"

"God has punished the people of Strasbourg for their sins but now he has forgiven them."

Antoine's tears continued to flow, but they were no longer of grief. They were of fresh anger, and bitter hatred for the man before him. The man who shut the people out of the church. The man who feasted while everyone else starved. The man who favoured the wealthy merchants over the farmers and workers. The man who killed his sister.

Antoine lunged forward and tackled Brother Thomas to the ground. He gritted his teeth as his hands closed around the clergyman's fleshy neck.

***

Adrienne's eyes fluttered open, the stone ceiling of the grotto swimming in and out of focus. A drop of water dripped onto her cheek as the blood returned to her face. She sat up, feeling the cool floor beneath her and looked around. Some of the other dancers had woken from their exhausted sleep and others were still unmoving. The last remaining victims of the Saint Vitus plague convulsed around the figure of the saint.

"Antoine!" she shouted, when she saw him grappling on the floor, Brother Thomas choking and spluttering beneath him. Her brother looked up, his hard expression vanishing instantly. A smile of relief spread over his face.

The clergyman seized his chance and reached for a rock on the ground beside him. He swung it at Antoine and there was a loud crack as his head split open, blood spewing from the wound. Brother Thomas backed away as the boy's body fell. By the time Adrienne reached her brother, the life in his eyes was gone. Crimson blood spread over the floor of the grotto, mingling with the blood of the dancers.

The statue of Saint Vitus looked on, tears streaming from its eyes.

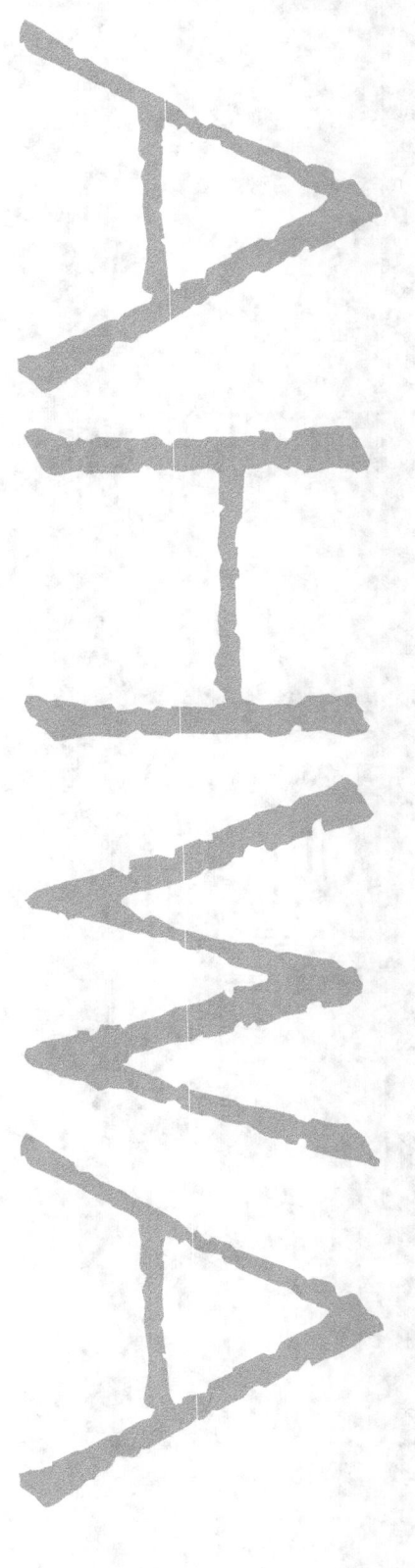

# THE RESTLESS SOUL

## BY FIONA L. RENTON

There is a place, if you look, where your soul can go to sleep.
It's not marked on any map, you must wait for death to creep.
But if you venture through the night, you'll find the depths of hell and more,
Where your soul can be redeemed, if you know how to settle the score.

Down the stairs, and through the dark, there's a corridor that leads,
Beyond the pillars of the old, and past the youth that pleads and bleeds.
There you'll find, upon the wall, just a key-lock, with no door,
And if your soul is dark enough, you'll find the steps beneath the floor.

Once inside, below the crypt, you'll meet the chamber of the damned,
And the scales of judgement waiting, for the Fool to play his hand.
There you'll place your beating heart, that you have cut from your own breast,
And wait for judgement to be cast, that you might lay your soul to rest.

For there, the payment must be made, not in gold coins, but pints of blood.
Your life regrets will count for naught, your tears, a dry and wasted flood.
Once the crimson drops are counted, and your deeds have been defrayed,
Then you can move across the veil, and see the choices you have made.

The gods of old will judge each life, reward for merit and curse for hate,
And deal a peaceful afterlife, or opt a painful reincarnate.
When your soul's weight has been lifted, and you're cleared to start anew,
You can begin a new beginning, with a you that has been un-youed.

# THE CARNIVAL GIRL
## BY LEANBH PEARSON
### WINNER OF THE 2022 ROBERT N STEPHENSON FLASH FICTION COMPETITION

Sunset lingered on the horizon as the carnival wagons approached the township of Well Springs. A wooden sign—paint peeling—swung from a dead tree and proclaimed two miles travel to the town.

In the lead wagon, Sylvie steered the piebald draught horse over the bridge and tried to ignore the bloated, crow-pecked corpse of a man also hanging from the tree. A crudely drawn eye slit was carved into the dead man's forehead. It was the symbol declaring him an Unnatural—like Sylvie herself—anyone attracted to their own sex.

She flipped the reins against the horse's back and continued along the road. Later, she led the Carnival wagons down the single street of Well Springs and squinted against the setting sun. The shopfronts lining the main street were all bordered up and as unwelcoming as the hanging corpse had been. The designated fairgrounds were empty fields wedged between the street and a dry riverbed. Sylvie shivered against the chill twilight breeze and directed the crew in their task erecting the main tent and the dozen smaller ones around it in a crescent.

First dark summoned the people of Well Springs to the Carnival. Sylvie sat at the ticket booth. She was familiar with towns like Well Springs—those who had succumbed to drought, lawlessness and war—now dominated by a cruel kind of people. She took their money in exchange for tickets and was careful not to meet anyone's eyes.

"What's a mermaid?" a young woman asked.

Sylvie looked down at the blonde before her, offering crumpled bills and waiting for an answer.

"Half woman, half fish. They sing so enticingly that sailors are lured to their deaths."

"The Carnival has one?" Her brilliant green eyes never strayed from Sylvie.

"We do." Her fingertips traced a secret symbol on the other woman's wrist as she passed the tickets.

She blushed. "I'll have to see her then."

"Last tent on the left," Sylvie chuckled, dark eyes sparkling.

Nodding in understanding to the unspoken tryst, the young woman smiled and disappeared into the crowd. Turning her attention back to the ticket booth, Sylvie tried to hide her own smile.

"I'll see this mermaid too." A broad-shouldered man thrust a handful of bills at Sylvie.

"Of course." She shuddered beneath his hard gaze and handed over a ticket.

She stayed at the ticket booth long into the night. She cast furtive glances toward the last tent but never saw the blonde woman or the man again. She'd travelled the Broken Lands long enough to be wary of Hunters—those who delivered a brutal fate to the Unnaturals.

The next morning as the sun cast bloody fingers across the dry pastures, Sylvie ordered the Carnival to pack up. She couldn't shake an unexplained sense of dread.

Anxious to leave Well Springs behind them, she encouraged the bicoloured draught horse into a trot with the rest of the Carnival wagons trailing behind her. She neared the dead tree on the outskirts of town and tears started to run down her cheeks. Try as she might, she couldn't look away from the young blonde woman hanging from a gnarled branch. A bloody eye slit carved into her forehead.

*Unnatural.*

Sylvie drove towards the next town. Outrage filled her heart, and a cold wind blew at her back.

## HE WAS ALREADY THERE
## BY JOSEPH TOWNSEND
### WINNER OF THE 2022 ROBERT N STEPHENSON
### SHORT STORY COMPETITION

### ONE

THIS EMPTY HOUSE, Letty Tice told herself, is just timber and brick—purposeless until someone has again taken residence.

And yet—walking up the long dirt driveway—where there'd once been gravel that would crunch under truck tires in the early morning—a wave of nausea passed through her.

The feeling one might get walking over a bridge and looking down into a chasm.

Seeing themselves falling.

### TWO

Bradley Little wasn't sure if he could do it. What would his father say?

*Rolling a stone over it won't keep it down, boy.*

His hands twisted around the splintered wooden handle of the pickaxe laid across his lap.

### THREE

White paint peeled from the clapboard. The front porch sagged. Shingles on the roof coming loose. Windows so streaked with grime they'd become opaque. The barn next to it— bowed in at the sides—walls gone the colour of soot.

Alone in an endless field of dead corn, blackened as if by flame, hanging limp from their stalks.

\*\*\*

The wooden floor, once polished, was now scarred and covered in a layer of dust so thick it seemed grey.

The stairs were falling apart—banister shattered halfway up, wooden poles sticking out an angle as if something had burst through.

A couch in the living room facing a brick fireplace, the kitchen beyond a black hole where flies swirled and bombed each other in hazy light through the fogged window.

Letty walked to the couch. Felt the fabric—sticky. She looked up—the ceiling had water stains—the paint peeling around it in a corona.

She walked to the window at the right of the fireplace. She looked out at the corn.

The sky was ashen, fading. She thought of snow.

### FOUR

John Tice found the footprints two months before his death.

The snow was fresh. The entire family, all four of them and the housekeeper, Muriel, had been on the front porch the night before watching it fall.

Letty was enamoured with snow. John

had watched her trying to catch the flakes on her tongue. He wasn't a particularly philosophical man—had been devoted to work his entire life—but recognized the constellations of thought and feeling behind his children's eyes, some essence akin to religious ideas of a soul, and that his watching them experience life in their way was a kind of communion with it.

None of them had left the house that night. John slept so lightly he would've woken if his wife stirred, or his children tried to creep out of their rooms.

Yet there they were. Footprints coming out of the corn.

The stalks were undisturbed.

The prints went towards the house, stopped at the back door.

He made a face, looked around. Nothing in all directions—nearest neighbour miles away. Town an hour's drive.

Perhaps Muriel had a lover come to visit in the night. The thought made his stomach twist.

He trod back to the front of the house, went to the kitchen. No snow on the floor. The door was locked. He stood there and looked out the window above the sink at the corn stalks swaying in the cold wind.

His light sleep was one of the reasons he'd wanted to move to the country. Quiet nights—undisturbed by traffic noise, sirens, neighbours heard through thin walls.

The first year at the farm he slept like a stone. But even in supposed silence, noise crept through. The rustling corn, stalks brushing against each other like tentative lovers. Animals in the barn. The owls.

He stood still, listening.

Later, before bed, he asked his wife about the prints.

She said that unless she'd walked in her sleep it wasn't her, and the children were too young to have planned a prank.

He brought up his theory of Muriel having a lover and they laughed about it—Muriel was too mean, Deandra said; if she had a lover he would be some scrawny submissive, not big enough to even make a dent in fresh snow.

Later on as they slept, the house creaked around them. The corn brushed softly. An owl far off made its' sound.

In the attic, a new noise—soft—a knife shearing slivers of wood.

### FIVE

Upstairs—pale rectangles on the aged wallpaper where there'd once been picture frames. A broken window at the head of the staircase —cold wind rattled the pane—made bumps rise on Letty's skin.

She went to Mikey's room.

Everything was gone save his bedframe— the wooden slats caved in, making the four-poster look like a collapsed crib.

She remembered sitting on the floor in that room, playing Monopoly. Colourful bills tucked under the board. He'd always picked the dog.

Muriel, their housekeeper, had been infatuated with Mikey. She'd called him 'Schätzchen'—little treasure.

She would stand in the doorway and watch them play. She would laugh at their silly voices, Mikey's antics—stealing money from his sister's bank or trying to surreptitiously move his houses or hotels when she was looking away.

Letty remembered the night Muriel left.

## SIX

Letty had been pretending sleep on the couch the night Muriel stomped into the living room wheeling a suitcase. Headlights flashed through the porch windows—an idling engine purred outside.

Deandra came down the staircase. Letty imagined her cinching her robe.

"Muriel," she said, breathless, "What's going on?" Who is that?"

The housekeeper had a thick German accent with a soft voice. "I'm terminating my employment. It is not a good place."

Her heavy shoes clocked towards the door. Deandra must've grabbed her by the arm because they stopped suddenly and Muriel made a noise.

"You intend to keep me against my will?"

"*Of course not, sweetheart.* Just take a breather. You're being…superstitious. Is this a German thing? I don't mean to be offensive, I'm sorry. I know it's frightening but it's been weeks, nothing has *happened*. It's old pipes, like John said. It's just *noise*."

Fabric rustled—Muriel shaking her arm free. On the couch Letty began to suck her thumb.

They batted it back and forth, Muriel staunch in her intent to leave, Deandra pleading, until finally the front door opened with a gust of cold air and Muriel said, "Gott segne dich," and walked out into the night.

Deandra swore.

John's voice startled Letty, from the stairs: "I can't believe this."

She listened to them comforting each other. She wished she wasn't pretending to sleep. She wanted to squirm between them and be held.

The car outside—tires on the gravel driveway, leaving.

She'd thought, we're all alone now.

## SEVEN

Her old room.

A small dresser underneath the window—pale blue blanket on the bed—toy chest at the foot.

Her legs were shaking when she stepped in on the creaking wooden floor.

Movement in the corner of her eye made her start—she fell against the open door and saw someone staring back with wide eyes -

Her reflection. A small mirror atop the dresser.

She looked at herself—blue eyes, strong jaw, shaved head.

Letty laughed—shaky. She ran a hand down her pallid face, over her scalp—felt the stubble—said, "When I leave, I'm gonna buy a pack of cigarettes," and laughed again.

She walked to the centre of the room—paused to set the mirror down on its face. Went through the drawers quickly—they were empty—ran a hand over the rough scratchy material of the blue waffle blanket.

She'd been drawn to the toy chest since crossing the doorway, knew she was putting it off.

Kneeling before it she felt the fine hairs standing at the nape of her neck. She took a deep breath, thought of the mindfulness practices she'd worked on in therapy.

She opened the chest.

A grey stuffed rabbit stared up at her with flat black button eyes.

Her throat closed immediately like an

allergic reaction. She shut her eyes until it passed and picked up the rabbit.

It was still soft. She gave it a kiss, set it aside. There were Legos, a battered Clue box. A brush still clotted with the blonde hair she'd once worn to her shoulders.

The backside of a picture frame caught her attention. She picked it up, turned it over.

Letty had the same picture at home, in an album: a photo of her as a baby, swaddled in a soft blue blanket, cradled by her mother's hand. She'd looked at that photo a few times —usually drunk—she'd cried over it.

This photo was the same.

But the hand was wrong.

The claw that gripped her infant body in the picture she held was old— gnarled with varicose veins—the nails black and yellow.

Strange vibration in her skull— like being in an airplane on descent—her ears popped and she swallowed and set the photo down.

The hand was familiar.

She knelt there trying to place it until a scream raised her head to the window.

From the barn—a horse—bellowing as if branded.

## EIGHT

After Muriel left, things around the house began to disappear—her father's newspaper would be gone and then found in the refrigerator, or a pair of shoes would wind up dangling from a corn stalk by their laces.

The noises got worse.

Thumps, like footsteps. Muttering.

John checked the cellar, the attic—found nothing.

One afternoon while the rest of her family was in town, Letty went out to the backyard. On the top step of the porch she found an oblong length of wood.

Smooth to the touch—big as a thumb. It'd been whittled.

Clutching it in her little hand she turned and looked up to the attic. She'd come to believe someone was up there.

The window that looked out on the backyard was opaque. It reflected only the blue sky and passing clouds.

## NINE

Walking out to the barn—Letty thought about loneliness.

She felt lonely by herself. She felt lonely with other people.

Her relationships—all failed—obsessive passion fizzled into cold distance.

It was in a fit with this feeling, drunk alone, that she'd dug up the police report— and for the first time read every word.

Re-living it sent her to the hospital to have her stomach pumped.

She got sober there, spent time in the rooms.

She got a therapist.

She told them what sent her over the edge: she remembered it all differently.

The therapist said, "The concept of universal truth is invalid. Memory is a choice. We need to process your trauma, Leticia, or it will keep affecting you—in ways you can't control."

In the police report, the night of her family's murder:

Her father had been drunk on the couch, sleeping. Her mother had been drunk in the kitchen, her head hung over a pile of bills. Her little brother had been trying to hide a set of soiled sheets—he'd been a chronic bed-wetter. Letty had been in the downstairs bathroom, fighting with the new housekeeper, Marla. She was trying to get Letty to have a bath but she'd wanted to stay up and watch a western with her dad, unaware that he'd passed out.

In Letty's memory:

John and Deandra were in the living room dancing to *I Want You* by Bob Dylan on the stereo. Mikey watched them from the couch, half-asleep. Letty had been with the housekeeper—Marla was showing her how to braid hair, using a Barbie doll as a model, the two of them laughing over it in the bathroom mirror.

When the record finished playing, and the needle rose and scratched the black vinyl surface to find the next groove, they'd all heard a thump—like weight falling from great height—and looked up to the ceiling, towards the attic.

### TEN

A horse bounded out of the barn as she approached. It seemed unafraid.

It cantered to a stop, snuffled. She stroked its silky neck. The horse's eyes were flat black, curious.

As if it'd only stopped as part of a larger errand the animal turned and galloped away—pushing itself through the corn.

Letty looked at the bent stalks. She took her pulse.

The barn's doorway was a black hole. She went into it.

### ELEVEN

When her therapist introduced hypnosis she was sceptical.

They sat her down. They brought out a metronome. Dimmed the lights.

Used their hand—two fingers—danced them in front of Letty's eyes, making them track.

Harsh click of the metronome.

Her breath.

The drone of their voice:

"One—you are not here. Two—you are not there. Three—you are not anywhere. Four—you are not here. Five—you are not there—"

Her eyes followed their fingers and began to feel heavy and she remembered a boy from school and his hot breath in the cafeteria when he leaned over and whispered about some game he was playing and she ran from him and her father found her and brought her home all wet and sick in the rain that time in May mother sick sat by her bed read stories and her favourite was Plath Mikey alone in his room Legos running in place legs pumping blood heart blood heart blood face wet syrup oh no god no stop please i don't want to i don't want to go back—

\*\*\*

She opened her eyes. She hadn't been aware of closing them.

The plane she looked upon was a deep black—pitted with craters, each filled with something white. She was naked and cold. The ground under her bare feet felt like chalk dust.

She knelt by one of the craters. The white substance reminded her of milk or semen. She touched it—gritty—no moisture.

A shape came up out of it—the white sluicing off as it rose—she couldn't tell what it was—it had a face—it submerged itself just as quickly and was gone.

She rose, walked on. The space above her head was incorporeal, lacking substance. The black around her seemed endless.

At a certain point she came across the child.

Crouched with its back to her—spine knobby and stark under pale white skin.

Its shoulders were hunched, undulating. Long blonde hair, nearly white, dirty and tangled.

It rose. A head shorter than Letty, slight.

She walked to it as if drawn by rope.

The child said, "I'm glad we finally met, Leticia."

Its voice was airy—aristocratic, used to being heard. It turned—wide blue eyes in a rounded face. Feminine features.

It raised its hands, gestured to the barrens all around them. "What do you think?"

Letty said, "I want to go home."

The child grinned. Her teeth were black and yellow, slick with saliva—strands of it, thick as snot, flowed over her bottom lip.

"You will," she said.

"I don't like it here…"

"That's awfully rude. I didn't complain about your house."

The child put her hands down. Old hands—gnarled—traced back to the forearms with thick varicose veins.

Letty said, "What do you want?"

"Go back to the farm, Leticia."

"Why?"

The child wiped her mouth with the back of her hand. She looked puzzled for a moment, then smiled. Serene.

"Because I said so."

"Who are you?"

The child shook her head slightly and turned, knelt again by the white crater.

She plunged her hands into it and raised up a cream-coloured sphere. It had flesh—

her fingers made indentations. She began to eat, smacking her lips, and Letty closed her eyes.

***

When she opened them the therapist was on his knees, shaking her shoulders. The metronome clicked in rhythm. She looked at the clock—two hours had passed.

He wanted her to stay—process—she told him it was fine—that it had been like being asleep.

After a restless night at home, she'd left for the farm.

## TWELVE

It was dark inside the barn.

There were four stalls for horses. A door beyond to the hatchery.

The floor was strewn with hay. She could see only so much with the lazy afternoon light streaming in behind her.

Her gaze was fixated on the second stall to the left.

A shadow growing—sound of rustling straw—something standing up.

The door began to creak open on rusted hinges.

Her breath caught. She recognized the sound.

## THIRTEEN

Bradley Little was born in Red Lodge, Montana.

He lived with his parents in an apartment above a drug store.

At night he would sit at his window and look down in the alley, watch cats dig through garbage.

He gave them names. Made up stories. They were his brothers and sisters. They were mythical. A pantheon of furred gods.

One day walking to school he found his favourite—Little Ann—lying still in the gutter.

He put her body in his closet.

He watched it rot for weeks.

He liked knowing it was always there.

When he turned fifteen his father died—an explosion at Smith Mine. Cause unknown. Seventy-five dead. His mother couldn't stand it. She went into her head, never came back.

After graduation he got a job at an abattoir. He liked to see the carcasses coming into processing—swaying on the hooks.

There was a man at work named Wyatt. Wyatt had a family. He showed Bradley pictures. One day at lunch he got too drunk and Bradley drove him home—after dropping him off he circled the block, parked a few streets away, walked in the dark back to the house. Hidden in a copse of trees he waited until morning and watched the family—two kids, a dog—the wife like a little fly buzzing around the kitchen.

He watched every day.

When he killed them all he used a knife.

Wyatt went first. He dragged the rest of them into the living room. He tied them up and made them look at their dead father then killed them one by one.

The little girl he did last. She reminded him of Little Ann.

He stayed in the house overnight with their corpses, sleeping in the same room.

In the morning he sat down on the couch in front of their arranged bodies and stuck Wyatt's .22 in his mouth with the barrel at the roof and pulled the trigger. The bullet ripped a jagged hole and bounced around inside his skull.

His head snapped back and he went somewhere else.

A black place, white holes in the ground.

Naked, scared, he explored until he found the child with the silvery-blonde hair crouched in front of a pool of what looked to him like white paint. She was eating something.

He thought of Little Ann—her soft white fur—blue eyes.

The child was kind to him—she understood.

She told him he wasn't done.

He came back still on the couch. He went into the bathroom—his chin and mouth were sticky, almost sealed with dried blood.

He washed his face, drank a glass of water—he could feel the cool liquid sluicing through the torn hole the bullet had made.

*** 

He came across the Tice farm in Illinois.

A piece of paper stapled to a corkboard outside the post office: "SEEKING HANDYMAN—FAIR PAY—WORK THRU FALL". It had the Tice farm's address, a phone number.

He drove past—saw the gravel driveway curling through the cornfields. He parked miles away in a dim grove and sat still until night. In the dark he crept through the corn—crows would soundlessly alight at his approach.

He watched the house through until morning—watched the Tice family go through their routine—the father making breakfast, the kids playing, the mother and the housekeeper tending to the animals.

He watched until the weather changed—snow—cold wind.

When the family went to bed one night he trudged through the fresh snow and went inside.

***

He found a crawlspace in the attic behind a pile of boxes. It was untouched. Tall enough to sit down, with a sheer drop at the end into the wall cavity. It smelled like mildew, rife with tangled wires.

He found a milk crate and tore insulation from the wall to make a seat.

The pickaxe he found in the barn—wandering while the family was in town one afternoon. It was light in his big hands.

They became aware of his presence as time passed. One month, two.

He couldn't leave. He wanted to leave. He couldn't stay. He wanted to stay.

He wondered if he could do it.

He never thought about why.

***

When the time came, he descended the stairs to the top floor of the house.

He went to Mikey's room first and with the squirming boy slung over his shoulder he found the rest of them.

John and Deandra didn't make a fuss. They collected Letty and Marla.

He marched them out the front door and down the porch steps and through the snow to the barn.

He put them in the stall. He tied them up, except for Letty. He sat her down in the straw.

John and Deandra begged. They cried.

He split their skulls with the pickaxe.

Letty didn't cry, or scream. She didn't try to fight.

As she watched her family and the housekeeper die screaming she reached up with her tiny hands curled into claws and began to rip out tufts of hair from her scalp.

The roots were bloody, like grass ripped from fleshy earth.

***

Bradley stayed in the house for three days. Letty never left the stall—he brought her food, fed her and the rest of the animals at the same time.

When the police came, they found her there—curled up under a blanket—ragged hair—in front of the frozen bodies of her family.

Bradley stayed in the corn, watching.

When they fanned out and began combing through the stalks he turned and went the other way.

***

When he came back to the farm months had passed and it was abandoned. They'd taken the girl and the corpses and they'd locked up the doors to the house.

The barn they left open. The animals were gone.

He went back to the stall and covered the blood stains on the concrete floor with hay.

He sat in the straw.

The girl from the black planet wouldn't let him go.

So he waited there and the years passed and they did not pass quickly for him, alone there in the creaking barn.

## FOURTEEN

kill worms are in me i feel them kill she's here i heard her yes kill

waited so long kill time kill stand kill see her face kill mattock heavy arms hurt legs hurt not hurt like kill hurt but different kill should oil the hinges kill why didn't that old man do it kill there she is kill kill kill kill

run short hair run why chase legs move run no light girl the girl girl girl fuck you no dreams all this time waited dyke CUNT

sorry kill so sorry kill i didn't think i would

no light half light house

little ann soft kill i held her kill i watched

run

hurt kill help kill

i just wanted to see my dad she said he was crying when the fire came out of the hole and i saw his face there and it was all wrong and melted like marshmallow i'm sorry please i'm sorry i think i know that smell same thing same fire don't do this

i think i'll sit down now thank you

kill kill kill sorry

sorry

i'm sorry

i never meant

to

do

this

## FIFTEEN

When Bradley Little sat down on the ruined couch, aflame, Letty dropped the barbecue lighter and sank to her knees.

The fire spread to the couch. The smell made her retch. The kerosene canister lay beside her—she slapped it away, her backside on the floor now, legs splayed out. The right knee of her jeans were ripped and the leg underneath was slick with blood.

He'd come out of the stall swinging the mattock and chased her into the house—thrown her from the stairs—she'd found the kerosene and the lighter by the old fireplace.

She didn't think she could walk—examined her leg, felt her hip.

The fire didn't seem to hurt him. He sat there like a monk and burned and the flames spread to the floor, licking their way to the walls and the staircase. The smoke was thick, rose to the ceiling.

Letty laughed—started coughing—knew she should start crawling to the door but a light had gone out somewhere inside and she just sat there trying to breathe.

Clattering sound of old wood—barely audible through the crackling flame—made her turn.

The child was crawling out of the fireplace.

Her arms were splayed out—scrabbling for purchase on the ancient wooden floor—the lower half of her body still in the chimney, wriggling.

Letty watched her slither into the room. The child laid on the floor a moment with her tangled blonde hair in a heap before twisting up to stand.

She walked to Bradley—put a hand into

the fire—her flesh began to sizzle, boils rising and popping as she stroked his blackening scalp.

"You did better than I could've hoped," the child said, and turned to Letty, grinning with rotten teeth. "The both of you."

Letty said, "What are you?" Barely a whisper, but the child heard and shook her head, smiling.

She crawled back to the fireplace. The fire had spread— she sat in it— hair going up, roasting off in wisps. She grinned and her eyes began to run out of their sockets like streams of pitch.

"You should get out," she said. "It would be boring if you died here, after everything."

### SIXTEEN

Letty crawled out of the house, made it to her car—called an ambulance before passing out on her back.

They found her there—burnt, bloody, alive.

They took her away.

The house burned. In the remains they found Bradley's bones.

Up late one night two detectives batted it back and forth and came to the conclusion that he was already there.

\*\*\*

Time in the hospital—skin grafts—rehab.

Her therapist came to visit—her roommate—an old lover—Letty couldn't speak.

When she got discharged they put her in a psychiatric ward—catatonic.

Pills to sleep—therapy.

Time passed.

At first none of it worked.

And then it did.

### SEVENTEEN

In the early morning dark she woke suddenly from a dream and sat up in bed, blinking slowly while her heart slowed down.

In a bathrobe and flannel pyjamas she went to the balcony. Her own apartment—no roommate—a view of the city, river twisting underneath a bridge, skyscrapers rising into grey clouds against a black sky.

She drank a cup of coffee and smoked a cigarette, flicking ash into the soft gusts of wind that buffeted her short blonde hair. Her phone sat on a round mosaic table—a text from her partner on the screen—"Hey, we still on for tonight?"

The dream—she remembered fire—pools of white—her bloodied hair. Old dream—familiar details.

She wondered about the child, if she'd see her again and when and why and if they'd meet in death come naturally or with intent and the fear came and went like wisps of smoke from the end of her cigarette and she flicked the butt away into the wind and watched it twist and fall and disappear entirely among the starlight of the city beneath and knew in that moment if she ever saw that black place again and the creature living in it she would wrap her hands around its throat and she would twist and hold until the evil light had gone out of its' eyes and she smiled standing there in the early morning dark with her blonde hair a curtain over one milky eye and knew the fear would come back—but one day it would not.

# BLOOD BORN

## BY PAULINE YATES

*Thieve from me or shirk the bill,*
*Bear a lifetime urge to kill.*
*If you try to end the curse,*
*Two plus you will grace the hearse.*

The curse torments my mind as I grab my car keys and push through the festering atmosphere in our house. Audrey sits on the couch, knees drawn, her white-knuckled fingers clutching her swollen belly. Empty potato chip packets litter the coffee table. She says that it's all she can stomach if she doesn't want to dry-heave over the toilet bowl. How she finds the strength to grow a baby when she barely eats, I don't know. But grow it does, as though desperate to escape before it becomes her next victim. After catching her in the kitchen adding drain cleaner to my coffee like a woman possessed, I share the same fear. I'm only alive because she needs me, for her and our baby. But the constant worry that in a moment of madness she'll forget I agreed to help her bear the curse is like walking on razor blades hoping not to get cut.

The offending book lies on the couch at her feet. I've asked her multiple times to put it out of sight, but she reads the curse on the inside cover over and over, trying to find a loophole. There isn't one, as we've discovered. She succumbed to the curse four months ago, the moment she walked out of the store without paying for the book. She claimed it was an oversight because of "pregnancy brain", and immediately tried to return it. Instead, she came home with the book in her bag and a blood-splattered dress. The dead store clerk with the pen shoved through his eye made news headlines for a week.

Raging pregnancy hormones and memory lapses I could accept, but murder because of a penned curse? I refused to believe an author's scribbles turned my gentle wife into a cunning killer. That changed when I found her standing over the bludgeoned gardener who she'd hired to mow the lawn.

Horrified to think my denial was contributing to the body count, I convinced Audrey to track down the author and demand he lift the curse. She recited the third line, *"If you try to end the curse"*, but I countered with, "What if the author himself is the loophole?"

It was a matter of choosing my words carefully. Audrey had changed under the influence of either hormones or the curse (I tried to tell myself it was the former)— and I didn't quite trust her. Or myself.

But she was surprisingly agreeable. Reaching up to kiss me on my cheek, and telling me how clever I was, she looked up the author's website, found his contact details, exchanged emails, and arranged a meeting on the pretence of buying more books in his collection, all within a week. Now it was my turn to tell her how smart she was, and how much I loved her. And always would.

We didn't even have to travel far; he lived an easy four-hour drive away. We made a bit of a road trip of it, like in the old days. But had it clicked that Audrey's enthusiasm to meet the author was driven by the curse, I would never have let her set foot on his property. The author, a pudgy bespectacled man with a receding hairline, didn't help by scoffing at us. Audrey was being hysterical, he claimed. I watched her eyes narrow at the word, saw how her knuckles tightened around her phone, and heard the crack of the plastic case, and my blood ran cold.

"The whole curse thing was just a gimmick to boost book sales," he said. "Funny how it kind of seems to have worked though!"

They were his last words.

Our meeting ended with another body to bury, and a new appreciation for how screwed we were. Trust might be out the window, but least we were in agreement about this; killing the author also slayed our last chance at lifting the curse had my loophole theory been true.

*** 

Out of options and with the baby due any day, I'm as enslaved by the curse as Audrey is.

I drive downtown to search for Audrey's next victim, where drunks loiter and the homeless huddle behind dumpsters. It's a pitiful existence, but the people here are more alive than I'll be if I don't uphold my bargain to help Audrey bear the curse.

This area is my usual hunting ground because it only takes a flash of a fiver to lure a victim into the car. But tonight, a steady drizzle clears the streets and washes the stink of vomit and piss into the storm drains. No one's around. Not even a stray cat.

I drive back toward the centre of town. It's nearly closing time for the local pubs. Someone might need a lift home. Turning down a side street, I pass Sammy's on Seventh. The urge to sit at the bar and down shots of aged whiskey hits me like a sledgehammer to the back of the head.

I need to just to sit and forget the curse, forget my purpose for being out tonight. I'd love to rip the offending book to shreds, burn every page, reduce the author's curse to ashes, and cast it over his dismembered remains, the bastard. But that would count as trying to end the curse, as Audrey pointed out. Think of the baby, she said. The baby, yes, but my god, what world are we bringing it into?

I need that drink.

I park on the adjacent street and return to Sammy's via the loading dock entrance. The overhanging roof at the back of the building offers protection from the drizzle. Mist rising from the tarmac curls around my ankles like the devil breathes on my feet. I've never really believed in such things, but now I wonder if he's behind the curse, for such a thing to exist can only be the work of evil. As disgusted with my actions as I am, only a coward blames the devil, and I refuse to be that, too.

I shove open Sammy's back door and descend a short stairwell. Sammy's is a basement bar, a haven for the lost and the lonely. It also provides the discretion I need as much as the drink. My mouth goes dry and I crave the liquor's numbing burn in my throat. I scan the room as I enter. The bartender chats with two patrons, regulars from how he addresses them using their first names. They both look dishevelled and defeated, one drink away from joining the drunks on the street. Easy prey, but I dismiss the thought. Regulars would be missed.

Neither pays me any mind as I sit at the dark end of the bar. The bartender flicks a grimy cloth around a glass and wanders my way. He eyes me up and down as though expecting trouble. Trouble, yes, but not here.

"What'll it be?" he asks.

"Whiskey. Double it up." I slap down a fifty.

He pours a double shot and slides it across the counter. I down it in one gulp and push it back for a refill. The whiskey burns like lava down my throat, but my body sucks up the heat. I consider tapping the counter for a third shot, but I shouldn't push it. A third will lead to a fourth and after that, I won't care about anything but finding the bottom of the bottle. That will lead to mistakes, and I can't make any.

I stand and point at the shelf behind the counter. "Give me three packets of those potato chips. The plain ones." That's the grocery shopping done.

The bartender tosses the packets onto the counter. Gathering them up, I cradle them in my arms *like a baby*, God fuck it, and leave the way I came. Fog replaces the earlier drizzle and the cold air slaps my face. Tugging my jacket around me, I head back to my car. As I walk around the end of the building, I collide with a teenager running full pelt from the other direction.

The kid bounces off me. He's dressed in a grungy brown sweater, wears a black baseball cap, and carries a flashy leather briefcase that doesn't match his attire. Hunter-me grabs his arm. Former-me relaxes my grip. The kid fends me off with the briefcase and continues running along the road.

I don't give chase. Killing kids isn't my gig, even though it's not actually me doing the killing, though it may as well be. But I'm still victimless and my anxiety spikes. I'm running out of time. If I don't find a victim, Audrey will order home-delivered takeout and I'll have a vehicle to dispose of as well as a body.

A man wearing a pinstripe suit and puffing like a steam train runs along the pavement. Reaching me, he stops and bends forward, clutching his waist as he catches his breath.

"Why didn't you stop him?" he asks. "Little blighter stole my briefcase."

I shrug. "Didn't fancy a knife in my neck. Lucky you didn't get one either."

The man grimaces and gazes along the empty street. "Dammit. Got my phone, my car keys, the lot." He wipes his balding head and looks around. "I should call the cops. Is anything open around here? I don't know this part of town."

"You missed Sammy's by a minute. Nothing else is open, either." Hating the liar I've become, I hold out the chip packets. "Wife's pregnant and got a hankering for these. I'm on my way home but can give you a lift to the station if you like. My car's parked across the street."

"That's mighty kind of you. As long as I'm not putting you out. I'm not married, but when my sister was pregnant, fried onion was all she craved. I'm Ted, by the way." He thrusts out his hand.

"Ben." I balance the crisps in one hand

and return the handshake. City fella by the feel of his silky-smooth skin; wouldn't know a hard day's work if it smacked him in the head with a shovel. "Come on. Let's get out here before we're both victims of a mugging."

I walk across the road, Ted in tow. Reaching my car, I open the front passenger door and wave Ted inside, then dump the packets of chips on the back seat. Running around the car, I jump behind the wheel and slam the door closed. My hot breath fogs up the window.

"Sorry, I'm making the seat wet," Ted says, wiping his hands over his damp trousers.

"Nothing a day of sunshine won't fix." I've forgotten what the sun's warmth feels like. Every day is gloomy now, clear skies or cloud. I start the car and turn on the heater. "Won't get you dry, but it will take the chill out of the air."

Ted holds his hands over the vent and rubs them together in the warm air. "Thanks. So stupid. I'm usually careful at this time of night, but I don't know this town and I walked the wrong way after leaving a meeting. Got myself all turned around trying to find where I parked my car. Do you work around here?"

"Civil engineer. My office is downtown, but I mostly work from home." My deceptive response is as subconscious as breathing.

"That's convenient. When's your wife due?"

"Any day now." I tighten my grip on the steering wheel, steadying myself for what's coming. "Would you mind if I stopped in at home first? You can phone the cops from there if you like. I don't want to leave my wife alone for too long, and the station

is a trip across town."

"Sure, sure," Ted says. "Read about it all the time, mothers getting caught out with quick births…"

He prattles on about his sister's emergency caesarean. I answer on autopilot, but my thoughts stray to Audrey. Needing to rush her to the hospital is our worst nightmare. What if her urge to kill strikes during labour?

I turn onto our street and drive to our house at the end of the cul-de-sac, a single storey brick construction hidden behind a steel fence. Grabbing the remote in the console, I open the gate, then the garage door once the gate closes behind us. The roller door slides up. A shovel, mop, and bucket stand against the wall inside. A shelf holds a pile of large garden waste plastic bags, an assortment of rags, and cleaning products; I make a mental note to buy more bleach. A chainsaw sits on the floor beneath. I keep it meticulously clean, but the silver chain grins like a maniac as the headlights sweep over it. Suppressing a shudder, I park and switch off the engine.

"Here we are," I say, opening my door. "The phone's inside. I'll find you a towel, too."

I get out of the car and collect the chip packets from the back seat. They're more a prop, now, ordinary everyday items that dispel any cause for concern. Not that it matters. Ted is right where I need him to be.

He gets out of the car and joins me at the door leading to the internal laundry, but pauses and looks at his muddy shoes.

"Leave them on," I say. "We ripped up the carpet and replaced it with tiles. Easier to clean once the baby arrives."

Ted chuckles and follows me into the

laundry. "My sister's house is all carpet and doesn't she regret not tiling? Her son's three now and she spends half the day trying to remove plasticine from the—"

A dull thud shuts off his voice. I spin around. Ted stands with his mouth agape, eyes wide and unblinking. Audrey stands behind him gripping a hatchet. The blade is buried in Ted's head. She pulls it out with a sucking squelch that churns my stomach. Ted teeters on twitching legs then collapses onto a basket of dirty clothes and rolls onto the floor.

I stare at Audrey, mortified. I knew she'd hear me arrive home, but hiding behind the laundry door and striking the moment we entered chills me to the bone. What if I'd come home alone and her need to kill made her forget her need for me?

Still clutching the chip packets, I raise my hands in defence. "Audrey, lower the hatchet. It's done. I'll take it from here."

She stares at me with a murderous glint in her eyes. Then a tear slips down her cheek, her fingers relax, and she drops the hatchet. It lands on the floor with a clunk, the handle resting against Ted's leg.

"The baby," she whispers.

A gush of fluid pours out from between her legs. Audrey gasps, then screams.

"The baby's coming." Contorted by contractions, she sinks to her knees.

Tossing the chips, I rush to her aid. Ignoring the reddish fluid pooling around her, I crouch and grip her shoulders.

"Let's get you to the bedroom." I can't bear the thought of birthing our child in the presence of a corpse. But Audrey shrieks again.

"It's coming, it's coming now." Panting, she rolls onto her back and fumbles with her clothes.

Pushing her hands away, I lift her dress and pull down her underpants. And touch the baby's tiny feet.

The blood rushes from my face. My body grows cold all over. A breech birth, a complication I hadn't considered. I lift my eyes to Audrey's. Her shocked expression mirrors my churning emotions.

"Get it out," she screams, then squeezes her eyes shut and bears down with a strangled moan.

My fingers are all thumbs. My heart punches my ribs. We'd discussed how we'd deal with the curse once we realised the malicious control it had over her; how I would deliver her victims and dispose of their remains. But we've talked nothing about what to do when the baby arrived, or how to handle birthing complications. My first thought is to call an ambulance, but I dismiss it. I've no time to dispose of Ted. Audrey needs me now.

Gripping the baby's feet, I tug while telling Audrey she's fine; the baby's fine; it will all be okay, even though we'll never be okay because of that damn book and that fuck of an author who thought it funny that the curse worked. He didn't laugh when Audrey grabbed his throat and squeezed until his face turned blue—

The baby's face is blue.

"The baby's blue," I shout and immediately wish I'd kept my mouth shut because Audrey snaps her head up and stares at me with wide eyes.

"Protect him," she whispers and stifles a sob.

"I'm trying to," I yell back.

She reaches out and grips my arm; her sharp fingernails bite into my flesh. "You don't understand. You must protect *him!*"

I yank my arm away. What the hell does

she think I've been doing for the last four months? Despite my efforts, our baby is blue, fucking blue.

My wife gives a final push and I catch the tiny body before it hits the floor. But my rush of joy at helping to birth our son snaps off with the appearance of the umbilical cord wrapped around his neck.

Ignoring Audrey's hysterical crying, I slide my fingers under the cord. It's tight, so tight, but I lift it over my son's blue face. I raise his lifeless body and pluck out strings of mucus from his mouth and nose. Cupping my lips over his, I blow air into his lungs. Once. Twice. Three times.

The baby splutters then his lips pucker and he mouths at the air.

Ravaged by another contraction, Audrey expels a sharp gasp then slumps and lies flat on the floor. Her legs twitch like Ted's did and her arms fall limp by her sides. Another head crowns, then a second baby rides a wave of blood onto the floor.

Snatching a dirty shirt from the laundry basket, I wrap it around our son, then scoop up his twin. It's a girl, and her umbilical cord trails to her brother—it was her cord wrapped around his neck. Untangling them, I bundle the girl into the shirt with her brother and lay them on Audrey's chest.

"Twins. And they're fine."

Audrey's gaze rests on the girl. "Protect him." Then she breathes out. But not in.

"Audrey? Audrey?"

Audrey's eyes glaze over. Blood pools under my knees, leaking from something that must have torn inside her. I want to save her, too, but there's so much blood spreading across the floor, she's beyond anyone's help.

Heart breaking as a light in my life dies,

I rest my head on her thigh. Emotionally drained, I can't say what I need to tell her, can't give her anything more than a whispered reassurance that she's free now; dying during childbirth won't count as trying to end the curse. It will die with her.

*Bear a lifetime's urge to kill.*

That's all she wanted.

To keep *him* safe?

My skin crawls. The boy whimpers, then opens his mouth and bawls. Hushing him, I sit up and study the girl. She stares at me through eyes so like her mother's. But that's not all she inherited.

Her eyes glint with the thrill of her first kill.

## SEA GLASS

## BY MASON HAWTHORNE

A cricket shrills in the night, high and harsh and with a broken, uneven rhythm. In the trees birds murmur as they settle in, and a fruit bat wheels overhead. Alice's hands shake as she takes the bottle of metho out of her bag. She fumbles a neat fold of paper from her pocket and squeezes it tightly into her palm as she checks the house number again, glancing around to make sure that she is alone.

It's a terrace house, with white render and the window frames and porch columns painted a darker colour in contrast. The garden is severe in its neatness; a row of roses which have been pruned down to the canes, and a strip of grass cut down to the roots. Behind the windows, she can't make out any light. Other houses in the row have the purple glow of a television screen, or the soft golden haze of lights. This one is dark.

Alice digs her sharp nails into the folded paper in her hand, and then she leans down to place it on the garden bed, between the two middle rose bushes. Her knuckle snags on a thorn and blood wells from the wound immediately, black against her pale skin. She holds her hand out over the rose bed, and the blood runs down her finger, beading at the tip of her fingernail, and she flicks it across the paper, the rose canes, the soil.

Gripping the bottle of metho with an injured hand is difficult. It takes longer than she'd planned to work the safety lid. Alice looks over her shoulder, along the road, but it is still and empty. Cars roll through the intersection at the bottom of the hill, but none take the turn. On the corner, an enormous dog sits, looking up toward her. As she looks, the dog stands and wags his tail. Alice turns back to the garden.

She pours the metho over the stubby rose bushes, the soil between them, the little wall bordering the garden bed. It sinks into the soil at first, and then pools and splashes, little droplets fly up to stain the hem of her skirt, and she takes a step back, trying to keep herself out of range. She tucks the empty bottle back into her bag, and takes a box of matches and an airplane sick bag from her pocket.

Alice closes her eyes. She takes a deep breath and then has to stifle a cough when the metho fumes hit the back of her throat. She takes another, more careful breath, centring herself. She strikes the match first try, holds the stick so that the flame grows strong and stands cleanly upright, yellow in the night gloom. The crickets keep up their sharp, insistent call. She flicks the match into the rose bed, right on top of the fold of paper, and the metho catches, with a *whoosh*. The little garden leaps into hot, colourless flames.

Alice doesn't stay to watch. With the sick bag gripped in one white-knuckled hand, she gets across the road before she feels the choking sensation in her throat, the awful squirm of a thick body clambering up her oesophagus.

The big dog that waited on the corner catches up to her, and presses himself against her hip as she walks. Alice doesn't break her stride as she lifts the sick bag to her mouth, and retches. Her eyes water, and her nose streams and something black and squirming tumbles out of her mouth and neatly into the slick plastic sack of the sick bag. Alice gasps for air, turns at the corner and continues briskly along, then ducks her head again, bringing up a stream of wriggling creatures, and then a heavy froth of round and slimy eggs. She spits twice into the sick bag, but even so, an egg bursts between her molars when she shuts her mouth, and she shudders.

By the time Alice and Caleb, the dog, get back to the main street, and take a turn down a narrow, winding supply street that runs along the rear of her home, Alice is clammy with sweat, and the little creature in the sick bag has given up trying to escape, and instead sits still at the bottom of the bag. Alice unlatches the creaky wooden gate, and lets Caleb in ahead of her, then steps through into the cool, quiet green of her tiny concrete courtyard. To her right, a tiny water feature burbles, and frogs cluster around it, hidden beneath potted ferns and the sprawl of a climbing passion vine, singing together. To her left, the wheelie bins, lined up against the wall, and then a profusion of plants in pots, and hanging baskets. Alice reaches out to run a hand through cool, soft leaves as she steps into the true darkness of the doorway, and

opens it without needing to see the key in her hand.

Caleb pads past her, and leads her down the short hallway that opens into the shop. From behind the beaded curtain that covers the door, Alice can hear a low, raspy voice singing; a mumbled, hesitating repetition of the same line, again and again, along with the chitter and scrape of broken glass being swept across the hardwood floor.

The singing stops when Caleb noses through the beaded curtain, and a moment later the sweeping stops.

"How'd it go?" Ariel is leaning on the broom handle, his long hair tucked behind his ears. Around him, the worst of the mess has disappeared while Alice was out, the shattered display case is gone, and most of the glass is swept into a neat pile in the middle of the floor.

"Fine," Alice says, holding up the sick bag, "haven't looked yet, though."

Ariel's smile is crooked, and the jagged line of his broken tooth is visible. "I'll get the book." He leans the broom against the nearest set of shelves and ducks behind the counter to extract the thick, glossy *Encyclopedia of Native Frogs*.

Alice takes a glass bowl from a shelf in the rear of the shop. It's intended for floating candles, a wide, flat thing with sides that curve inward a little at the top. She pours some fresh water into it, and carefully upends the sick bag over the mouth of it. A slurry of frog spawn and tadpoles—looking sluggish from being so long out of water—plop into the bowl, and finally, after she gives the bag a bit of a shake, a big frog tumbles in.

Ariel whistles through his teeth, and turns on a lamp. In the yellowish light from the dusty bulb, the frog's blue-green back and golden eyes shine. "Nice one," he says, "don't even need to look that one up. Beautiful."

"Green Tree Frog," Alice says, "I was hoping…" She turns away from the frog in the bowl, and from Ariel, and from Caleb, who has padded over to peer through the glass at the little creatures swimming inside.

"Well listen," Ariel says, "any one of these taddies could be an endangered one. And there's heaps of eggs in this lot." He smiles his crooked smile and bends down to look at the frog eye-to-eye. "Don't count your eggs out 'til you've, uh, counted them."

Alice turns and looks at the rest of the shop, the semi-precious stones strung from the ceiling, the glitter of gems and silver in the jewellery cases. She lifts her glasses onto her head, and presses her hands over her face, mindful of her make-up.

*** 

When she was twelve, wading in the clear, shallow sea water at Slaughter Beach, her bare feet tender on the floor of rounded stones, and one arm busy catching up the skirt of her cotton sundress. That long ago, she hadn't ever thought a thing about crystals, except to admire the large purple one her aunt wore on a leather thong around her neck. She liked the colours, and the cool crisp lines of the way that the stones formed. But mostly the colours.

There she was on the beach, the sun falling heavy across her narrow shoulders, etching the shape of her dress's thin straps into her skin, burning hot against her dark hair, picking out the line of her centre part, so that for weeks afterwards she'd be sore, and then itchy, and then covered with

flakes of peeling skin, the worst sunburn of her life in a stripe right down the middle of her head. The sun was hot, the sky a cloudless enamelled blue, and the water was so clear and clean that she could see the bottom, and her pale feet under the water, and the little scraps of seaweed that floated about her ankles, and the smooth white shapes of shells, half hidden among the stones.

Among the stones, and the shells, there were bright little glimmers of colour, deep greens and rich, glowing yellow-browns, the occasional brilliant blue. Alice trod through the shallows, eyes scrunched tight against the glare of the sun off the lapping water, and she bent down to collect them, pretty as gems, but worn into smooth, rounded shapes by the motion of the water rolling them against the sea floor. There was a little square pocket on the front of her dress, purely decorative, but she placed each brightly coloured fragment into the pocket so that it stood out against her chest, the lacy sunflower motif straining with the load.

She was bending down, feeling through the stones for a bright green when the shadow fell across her.

"Collecting sea glass, darl?"

Alice looked up, holding the green piece tight in her palm. The man was a stranger; old. Older than her aunt, at least. He wore speedos and had goggles strapped across his forehead, and he stood leaning down with his hands braced on his knees, so that his face was close to hers. Alice didn't move except to nod, carefully.

"Aw, you're a very good little girl, aren't you?" He smiled, and his teeth were crooked and yellow. His face was red and crumpled, his whole body was red and crumpled, and covered with shaggy white hair, curling across his shoulders, and in a pelt over his chest and belly. He was not fat, but large, like a footie player. His approval lay across her shoulders, as heavy as one of his thick hands. "How many colours have you found? Y'know that's glass, right? Glass from bottles. The brown ones will be your beer bottles, or maybe your ginger beers, and the green is from your ciders, and the blue ones are them Evian waters—never used to see much blue." He grinned, and Alice ducked her head, looking at her feet under the water, stomach churning.

"You're a very good girl. Picking up rubbish like that. It's good for the environment," he bent his head lower, trying to push his face into her line of sight. "Where's your mum and dad? Hm? Are they keeping an eye on you?"

Something cold clutched Alice's throat, and she curled her toes against the pebbles under her, and gestured toward the beach. Her eyes were watering, and if she turned her head she probably wouldn't be able to pick her aunt among the trees that shadow the steep basin where Slaughter Bay is nestled. She tried to say something, but she couldn't make her mouth open.

At last, the man stood upright, shaking his head as though he was disappointed. "Well I'll let you get on with it," he said. Then he snapped his goggles over his eyes and dived out into the water, sending a wave that buffeted Alice's legs and splashed up to wet her sundress.

Alice dropped her skirt, and clapped both hands over her mouth. She bent over the water, her own warped reflection squirming on top of the gentle swells. Coughing into her cupped hands, she caught something hard and sharp-edged, a crystal, white at one end, and a dark amber at the other.

When she showed the crystal to her aunt, and told her what happened, her aunt only sighed and shook her head, one hand touched the crystal on its leather thong around her neck. "Poor little pet, I thought it'd come down to you sooner or later. I hoped I'd be the last one. Tomorrow I'll take you to the shop, and we'll have a talk about it. How are you feeling? Is your throat sore?" Alice, twelve years old, clutched the stone in her palm, with her wet sundress clinging heavy about her legs, and burst into tears.

\*\*\*

Alice rubs her eyes, smearing her carefully applied eyeliner, and dislodging flakes of mascara. She settles her glasses back onto her nose and looks at Ariel, still peering into the bowl at the frog. "I don't know about this," Alice says. She's tired.

"Well…" Ariel says, "I guess you don't have to know. Not for sure, at any rate."

"What does that mean?" Her voice is sharp, she doesn't have Ariel's ease with ambiguity. She can't see good in bad, and bad in good like he can, as though he's turning over a coin.

Ariel laughs, "Doesn't mean anything. But I don't think that the guy who trashed your shop was having a crisis of self-doubt at the time."

"But that doesn't mean that I can just throw curses around."

"Well you said that he said you already cursed him. Wasn't that how the whole thing started?"

"He did, but I didn't. And I think it started a couple of months ago."

"What happened a couple of months

ago?" Ariel takes the broom from where he'd set it aside, and leans on the handle, head tilted.

"I refused to sell him human remains."

"Seriously?"

Alice steps behind the counter and picks up a handful of crystals, weighing them in her hand. "From there he just started saying wilder things, like he said I cursed him and that's why he was losing his hair, or why he got a parking fine."

"And you only just now decided to do something about it?" Ariel whistles, "maybe he was giving you suggestions, maybe he really *wanted* you to curse him?"

Alice closes her hands around the crystals and turns, looking at the rest of the shop, the crystals hanging from the ceiling, the jewellery and the semi-precious stones. So little has changed since that day when her aunt brought her here to stay, explained how things worked. Or how she thought they worked, at least.

*It's not what you do. It isn't diamonds for good little girls, and frogs for nasty little girls,* her aunt told her, *It's the judgements people make. You can't let them get to you. Let them roll off you. And you can't judge yourself too hard, either.*

Well, Alice can't stop judging herself. She can hold her judgements in her hands; her small acts of kindness glitter coldly from every surface of the room, they tear her throat and leave her hoarse and spitting up blood. Her cruelties, however, have lives of their own, they crawl out into the world, they live and multiply. The green frog in the bowl has placed his pudgy little hands on the glass, and peers at her with one round, gold eye.

So little has changed. But now she has a friend.

"Do you want to know what I put in the curse?" Alice says, her mouth curling.

Ariel nods.

*"It is exactly what you think it is,"* she returns the crystals to the shelf, arranging them into neat rows.

"Okay, that's pretty funny."

"Well, it's like you said. If he's going to keep accusing me of things I didn't do, I'd hate to disappoint him."

# NO RETURNS

## BY PENNY DURHAM

*● ● ●* *And finally this week, Last Gasp wants to salute the tenacity, the sheer brazen refusal to take no, of one Malison Carswell, self-styled witch, high priestess, psychic healer, health alchemist—and, naturally, fervent anti-vaxxer.*

*Ms Carswell has submitted for our serious consideration here at MedExpress her treatise on healing, titled Towards an Arcana of Wellness, not once but three times, and since she has ignored two polite rejections, we hope this one might get through.*

*Ms Carswell: extraordinary claims require extraordinary evidence. Take it up with Sagan, we don't make the rules. In your 3000-word article—which the whole MedExpress office has now tried to read, resulting in a range of migrainous symptoms—not a jot of evidence is adduced for your claims to "cure cancer without chemo, heal hypertension without beta blockers, reverse obesity without Ozempic and decrease depression drug-free" (though we do appreciate the amazing alliteration).*

*The article is a fantastical hodgepodge of unsupported assertions, seemingly drawn from the superstitions of every culture on earth, without even one independently documented case study.*

*Don't even start us on the grammar, which is as esoteric as the subject matter.*

*We are a medical publication, Ms Carswell, and we won't be promoting mystical practices that entice sick people away from effective, even if unpleasant, therapies—practices that, to judge from your website, will cost them just as much as the ones that work. Try Woo Weekly.*

\*\*\*

"Spicy column, Pol."

"Yep. I'm sick of that nutter. She'll have to get the message now."

"You don't think she'll sue us?" winced Lauren Ware, a junior reporter fresh from a media law course.

"Pfft. Bring it." Under her bravado, Polly Dunning, *MedExpress's* editor, quietly wondered if she'd gone a bit far in her Friday roast of the week's news and nonsense. She hadn't done a media law refresher in years.

"That naturopath case is still ongoing. The GP with the YouTube—"

"Yes, I know. I don't think I wrote anything she could really go us for, though. And please, don't ever say 'still ongoing' in copy."

"She is pretty intense. What sort of name is 'Malison' anyway?"

"Google's a thing," growled Harry Dolan, the tech guy, from the corner of the office.

\*\*\*

Amid Tuesday's mail pile of magazines, fliers and circulars was an envelope addressed to Polly, stamped Strictly

Confidential, with the enticing bulk of a thumb drive inside it.

Inside was a brief typed letter, without a sender's address or signature, that read:

*I work at the Department of Health and I've seen your FoI request. They won't give you the documents, but your readers need to know, so here they are.*

A whistle blower—brilliant! Polly's heart fluttered as she fished the USB stick out of the envelope. She didn't know which of their several outstanding FoI requests this referred to, and it might be dangerous to use the material, but if someone felt strongly enough to leak it, they must be on to a cracking story.

It was only as she plugged in the USB and her computer whirred that her brain flashed up a warning—*uh-oh … malware*—and by then the screen had gone black.

Two words appeared at the top, large and all-caps: *THREE WEEKS*

Beneath there was an animation. A face that might have been her own by-line photo—it happened too fast to be sure—disintegrated, its skin sloughing off, muscle shrivelling down to bone, until only a grinning skull remained.

"Fuck!" Polly yanked the stick and the power plug out of her desktop computer. "Shit shit shit. Harry? Help, please, I'm an idiot."

Harry sighed and tugged his beard. "What have you done?"

*\*\*\**

That evening, after an investigation that found files intact and no sign of further contamination in the office computers, Polly left for home. She liked to walk the 40 minutes from the office to her flat, even in the winter's early dark, as it served both

as exercise and as a buffer between work and home. The route was well peopled and safe.

This night, however, she had a persistent feeling that there was someone following her at a short distance. There was nothing so regular as footsteps, just an occasional skittering noise behind her on the pavement; and when she turned back to look, she could see only a flapping whiteness in the corner of her eye that swung away or melted whenever she tried to look at it directly.

Mostly the presence was behind her; once or twice it appeared on the other side of the street, level with her eye, hopping and moving erratically.

I'm just tired, she reasoned, rubbing her eyes. She kept her gaze fixed forward, not turning around the rest of the way home.

*\*\*\**

The next morning an email came from a friendly doctor contact with two "urgent" exclamation marks and the subject line: Your column.

*Hey Polly,*

*Hope you're well, I'm baaack from ICGP in Ottawa, landed last night—I can write something up for ME if you like?*

*But the reason I'm emailing is that I've just caught up with your Last Gasp from Friday and thought I'd better warn you that Malison Carswell is not a nice person. Even in the alt-med community she has a bit of a nasty reputation, she holds grudges apparently. I don't think she's the lawsuit type but you may still want to take out that bit about her, she may not have seen it yet?*

*I say this because a GP I used to work with wrote about her on his blog, basically saying she was full of shit and a danger to the public, and, well it's going to sound funny and this may be total coincidence but he wasn't himself afterwards. He lost weight really fast, his mood changed, he became jumpy but wouldn't explain why, though I remember him mentioning her name. Then he stopped coming in to work. About maybe a month later he died quite suddenly, supposedly from an undiagnosed cardiomyopathy, which I thought at the time was pretty weird. He was only 43, lovely guy—here's the* <u>link to his blog</u>*…*

The email gave Polly a small pang of nausea. She was not backing down, she insisted to herself as she opened the WordPress page for the Last Gasp column and deleted the section on Carswell. Nor was she scared. She was protecting the business from legal action.

The column had been online for four days and had clocked up a few thousand reads.

To distract herself from thoughts of Malison Carswell in the minutes before the 10am pitch meeting, Polly turned to one of the tech blog pages Harry had helpfully sent her about the risks of #badUSB— a kind of threat that had been around for at least 10 years, he'd said, shaking his head.

As she was trying to understand a sentence about microcontrollers, keystroke injection attacks and data lines, an ad on the right of the screen caught her eye.

The vertical box showed a man's face, with the text: "R.I.P. Gordon White, FRACGP, of Cherrybrook, NSW. Died 18 September 2021. Three weeks were allowed."

There was no other information, making it the oddest ad Polly had ever seen. Wondering what ad-targeting fail had caused it to be served to her, she clicked the X in the top right to bring up the 'Stop seeing this ad' option. But the box just migrated to the centre of the page and wouldn't budge. Its imprint remained after she shut the browser tab and the browser itself, and only when she restarted her Mac did it go away.

As she waited for the computer to reawaken, Polly thought about the name, and the postnominals. She opened the email from the GP and clicked on the link. Medsceptic.org.au was "A blog about health sense and nonsense" by Dr Gordon White, Sydney GP, now with a tribute placed prominently on the home page. The face that smiled from the About page was the one in the "ad". His final post, "Deluded or a charlatan? Either way, she's preying on the vulnerable", was in August 2021.

"You ready to go in?" Lauren was hovering, her face concerned again. "You feeling OK?"

"Fine. Let's do it."

The next morning Polly shuffled, blinking, into the bathroom. The sight of her own face in the mirror startled her awake: it was covered with wafers of loose dead skin, translucent and white, like peeling old varnish on weathered timber furniture. She took the edge of one flake and lifted the dead skin off easily. Then another, then another. Then she ripped a papery layer off her forehead and screamed as a slab of fresh skin came away between her fingers, leaving a raw, pink wound.

Breathing hard and trembling, she smoothed the flap back down and looked in drawers for a dressing. After showering carefully, and getting dressed even more carefully, she made her way to work, ignoring the curious glances on the bus and in the coffee queue, evading questions in the office.

But it was hard to concentrate on work. Gentle office chatter was like the din of snarling dogs; the fluorescent lights made her eyes water; stories were unscalable walls of words.

The deputy editor Charlie Locke took her aside in the early afternoon. "Pol, are you feeling all right?"

"Fine. Why?"

"Well … it's just that I've had to correct a few things you published this morning, which I never normally have to do. Some were just a few literals, you had 'witch' for 'which' and 'curse' for 'course'. One headline, though, the one about that aborted dementia drug trial, it was all arse-about. Instead of 'Trial ends after three deaths in a week' you had 'Three-week trial ends in a death.'"

Polly blinked at him. "I wrote that?"

"I'm afraid so." He looked pointedly at her forehead.

"Oh— no. I haven't had a head knock, if that's what you think. Just a … cat scratch. Got a bit infected. But I think you're right, I might go home, if you can look after the afternoon send?"

Charlie nodded. "Of course. Rest up."

As she walked out, waving tight goodbyes, Harry swiveled in his chair and opened his mouth as if to say something, but then closed it again.

*\*\**

Polly felt both exhausted and on edge when she reached her apartment, which she shared with a tortoiseshell named Millicent. She'd walked home again, for the air and sunshine, hoping it would clear her head, and there was no sense of pursuit.

But as she crossed the threshold into her flat, she immediately felt observed.

The sense was strong enough that she went through each room, twitching aside curtains and throwing open wardrobes, but nothing was amiss.

Polly gave Millicent an early dinner and apologised for defaming her to her colleagues. The wound on her forehead throbbed, but she couldn't bring herself to remove the dressing and see what state it was in.

She tried a book, then television, to fill in the afternoon that yawned ahead, but couldn't focus on either. Eventually she took her book to the nearest park and stayed there, mostly not reading, till it was dark.

Back in the flat, determined to ignore the undoubtedly imaginary feeling of eyes on her, she cooked spaghetti, but then threw most of it in the bin and went to bed. Her exhaustion did not convert easily into sleep, however, and she lay for an unknown span of time in a cycle of slipping into a dream, realising it was a dream and waking up, then slipping slowly back.

The dream was always the same. She was walking what must be her normal way home, though the houses were more pointed somehow, the streets more twisting, and something was following her. She started to jog, took a route through back streets, but could not lose her pursuer; then chose to leave the streets altogether and creep through the gardens of the houses, scaling wall after wall until she grew tired, then exhausted, and all the while something was gaining on her, its ragged movements getting closer. Every time she woke up and drifted off again, the whole sequence would start at the beginning.

After what felt like hours of this, Polly reached for her phone in the darkness beside her to check the time, but fumbled and dropped it into the space between her bed and bedside table. Reaching down for it, she plunged her hand into what she would later swear was a mouth, with teeth and a long smooth tongue like a dog's, but which closed around her fingers with rough lips and sucked.

Polly was out of bed and through the balcony doors on the other side of the room before she was aware of having moved. She stood there not breathing, listening for noises from the room over the drum of her pulse. There was no sound. She wanted to put the light on, she wanted to wash her hand, but both would mean walking past her bed; so she just crouched there, shivering on the small balcony, till first light. As the sun entered her bedroom, so did she, to find her phone lying in the gap and nothing else.

Polly collapsed on the bed and slept, dreamlessly, through her alarm, finally waking at 9.30 with a jolt and hurrying in to work.

\*\*\*

There she found a commotion. Someone had broken in and tossed the place, opening every drawer and rifling papers on desks, but not stealing anything as far as they could tell. The police had come and gone by the time Polly arrived and had been visibly baffled by the lack of obvious break-in signs and the failure to trigger the building's alarm systems. They shrugged and recommended an upgrade.

As the other staff buzzed with speculation as to the intruder's purpose, Harry sat quietly in the corner.

When the call of deadlines forced the resumption of regular work, he messaged Polly on Slack: "Can I grab you later to chat about something? Get a beer at the Arms?"

The Stuart Arms was the further-away pub where Express staff didn't usually drink.

"Sure. Think I know what it's about."

\*\*\*

"For starters, you look like shit."

"Thanks, you're a darling." She caught sight of herself in the angled strip of mirror over the bar. Even in that small, distorted reflection she could see the wound on her forehead oozing strange colours through the dressing.

"No, really. Can I ask what's been happening? I don't know what kind of cat you have but … it's kind of obvious you're not right."

Polly took a deep breath, said "OK, fuck it", and told Harry about her week, including the email about Gordon White. He puffed his cheeks and let the air escape slowly.

"What do you reckon about that break-in?" he asked after a moment.

"God knows. Weird though."

"Right? I think they may have been after this." He produced from a pocket a small baggie containing the thumb drive she had received on Monday, with its innocuous casing of plain purple rubber. He held it between finger and thumb, as if not wanting to touch it any more than necessary even through the plastic.

Polly just raised her eyebrows.

"OK, look. I took this home to play with—no, trust me, my home setup is … pretty advanced." He made an OK sign and clicked his tongue. "I looked at the code and found what you described— the words and the schlocky animation with a jpeg of you, which they must've taken right off our website. Then there were some completely gobbledegook symbols in the code, not even ASCII, I don't know how they even got there.

"Then at the end there was a self-destruct exe file, but I think you yanked the stick out too fast for it to execute. Well done on that, at least."

"Yay me. What does any of that mean?"

"How closely did you actually read Malison Carswell's article before you smashed it in your column?"

"There was some skimming involved."

"Well, I read it carefully." This was a little supercilious. "Do you remember the bit about throwing hexes? She said she only used them for healing, of course, and that they could be done remotely."

"Like telehealth but with witches?"

"Sort of. She doesn't trust email, prefers a physical object, but postal services work."

"So. You think she's hexed me through that thumb drive." Polly snorted, but felt a rush of relief at saying the words out loud. It was absurd, and the only thing that made sense.

"Think about it. You publicly trashed her work. She's a grudgy person. Your weird shit started after you opened this. The other guy …" He stopped. "The code was meant to be irretrievable—why? Maybe so it couldn't be sent back. No returns. We had an impossible break-in, which I think was a failsafe to get this back in case the self-destruct didn't work. But I *did* retrieve the code—and I think we *should* send it back. And we're on the clock."

"I don't know her address."

Harry scoffed. "Some journalist."

"OK fine. But how can we persuade her to open something like that? Won't she be on her guard?"

"That's your job to figure out and write the copy for. She got you good with that FoI snare, and you're not the biggest idiot I know. There must be something she wants enough. I can get a new custom thumb drive made up to look like anything."

"Does she need to click on something or just plug it in?"

"Did you click on anything? No—it executes on connection."

"Right." Polly sighed. "Wait a minute, listen to us. This is nuts! I don't believe in any of this."

"You think I do? Here's a decision tree." He drew forking lines with his finger on the table. "Either we proceed on the basis of what's scientifically possible, or we go with what's actually happened and return this hex to sender. Option A outcomes are 1) nothing happens and all this spookiness goes away, or 2) you develop a fatal heart condition or the world's fastest-growing cancer and in two weeks' time it's bye Polly. With option B either 1) it's a harmless prank that costs us a bit of work to pull off or 2) … Carswell gets a taste of her own medicine."

After a minute Polly nodded.

"All right then. You have homework. It's Friday, so about 17 days till deadline. The drive'll take a few days to get made, and we have Australia-fucking-Post to factor in, so work out your snare and have it to me by Tuesday."

Over the next two weeks Polly spent as little time as possible either at home or alone, staying with friends and cousins for a day here and there, eventually moving with Millicent and a small bag of clothes to Harry's windowless basement flat. If the rest of the office suspected anything was going on between the 45-year-old editor and the ponytailed late-20s IT guy, they were too polite to ask.

Polly drafted a letter and gave Harry instructions for the custom USB. She had had the designer create a letterhead and logo, saying it was for a story on predatory journals.

They found an image of Carswell online: she was middle-aged with long bleached hair and a thin mouth, kohl applied like crayon around her pale blue eyes. Harry substituted it for the jpeg of Polly in the code, just in case that was a load-bearing part of the hex—though from what he had read in her treatise, he said, the photo was just window-dressing; the act of connecting the device and executing the program was what mattered.

By the end of the second week they were ready. Then they waited.

During this time dread hung about Polly like a shawl. She became used to its weight pulling at her thin shoulders, and grew to expect the intrusions of strange shapes into her peripheral vision. She couldn't watch TV, because wherever she wasn't looking on the screen there would be a chalky apparition that vanished when her eyes flicked to it. She could not eat more than a mouthful or two of food a day before her meal turned from pasta into a plate of centipedes, or from a sandwich into a handful of rotting flesh with the fur still attached. She was tired all the time but afraid to sleep because of the dreams.

Charlie quietly took on more and more of her work.

But as the third week got under way,

Polly felt the pall begin to lift, and the occurrences grew rarer. By the Friday, the day they had chosen to post their package—wanting neither to miss the deadline nor to be too early—she felt a kind of elation mixed with the severest case of butterflies she had ever known.

The pair slipped out of the office at lunchtime, walked to the nearest post office, put the envelope in the slot, and withdrew to the Arms for a beer—not to celebrate, but to settle their shaking hands. After a long silence Polly said: "It still doesn't feel right. Despite everything."

Harry just nodded.

***

*Dear Ms Carswell,*

*The Journal of Western Esotericism is a peer-reviewed academic publication devoted to the study of traditions including alchemy, astrology, Gnosticism, magic, mysticism and spiritual healing.*

*We have been reliably informed that your article entitled Towards an Arcana of Wellness is an astute and original piece of research and would like to be the first to publish it, if you have not already found a home for it elsewhere.*

*We charge an author fee of USD750, significantly less than some of our competitors. Payment instructions are below.*

*Please upload your article as a Word document with references in APA style to the enclosed USB device and post to the address above. (We do not accept email attachments for cybersecurity reasons.)*

*Yours sincerely, …*

Malison Carswell beamed. At last, the academic recognition she was due. The only pity was that the woman from *MedExpress* wouldn't be alive to know about it. It was almost worth recalling the … but no, it was done.

"Mephista?" she called. "Miffy? Come in here a minute, darling. Can you help me with something on the computer?"

Her 15-year-old daughter, IT person and secretary, shuffled into the study looking put out.

"What."

"I need you to put my article on this thing here. Then put it in an envelope and address it to these people. Can you do that while I get dinner on?"

"Kay. Get off, let me sit."

Mephista took the drive from her mother's hand. After a glance at the official-looking logo, satisfied, she plugged it in to the slot.

# HIKING THROUGH THE FUCKING OUTBACK BECAUSE YOUR THERAPIST THINKS YOU NEED NATURE

## BY KATE POZZOBON

His therapist suggested this. And, yeah, he's seeing a therapist. Marianne. Found her with a quick Google, a scroll, a click. Not about to release that info to the big wide world, but he thinks there's some song material there. Maybe a whole album. Enough to bring him out of this rut he's found himself in. Same old song and dance as every other failing rockstar: the booze, the blow, the babes all were too delectable and that's where money and muse find themselves wasted on.

A pit. A volcano. Everything sucked vortex deep.

That's a good line, too, he thinks. Squirrels it away for this hiking slash therapy slash comeback album he's got percolating in his mind. Working title: *Witch's Brew*. Working song: "Hiking Through the Fucking Outback Because Your Therapist Thinks You Need Nature."

The latter will need work shopping. God knows he's got the time.

Billy's never been a backpacker or a hiker or even a weekend bushwalker. Remembers taking the odd trip with his mum when she was in one of her good, need-to-be-a-quality-mama moods. They didn't live far from bushland, and Billy distinctly remembers the smell of eucalyptus trees and stagnant rivers. At the end of it Mum would always be in a bad mood for some reason or another. A sour taste left in Billy's mouth. Writing it off as Bad Memories. Bad Things.

So it's safe to say he's not an outdoorsy guy. Never even tried drugs until he was rich enough to get them delivered *Uber Eats*-style to his hotel room. He wonders if any finance guru has written about that sort of lifestyle creep.

"Finance Guru."

"Lifestyle Creep."

Better titles. See, he's been out here less than an hour and he's already got three song ideas up his sleeve. Maybe this three-hundred-bucks-an-hour therapist is on to something.

Billy starts humming something, but the instrumental side has never been his forte. Tried them all, everything from guitar and drums to the more obscure bagpipes and harpsichord. Nothing stuck. Reading music was beyond him. It was the words that came easy, and maybe he was built more as a poet than a rockstar but who's getting that rush of a thousand drunks screaming and cheering at a local library poetry reading?

Billy knows fame's the true drug he's always been chasing. The one he can always picture but never take hold of. His stomach grumbles at the thought, mouth salivates. He keeps walking because that's what he's been told to do.

It's early winter but Billy's already sweating down his thin cotton shirt, rivers getting stuck under the straps of his backpack. He's unfit, stacked on the pounds with his diet, trying to lose it all which is why he picked this out of his therapist's half dozen suggestions. Maybe he can get that emaciated rock-star body back. Strut around the stage shirtless, bras and underwear from female fans tossing themselves at him. Those were the good old days. The long, long gone good old days.

Yeah, yeah, and maybe you'll land a two million record deal. Keep dreamin', Billy. You were always cursed to be small news. Old news. Forgotten, chewed-up-by-the-dog news.

He's thinking all these self-deprecating thoughts and trying to build a song out of them when he spots it. Or rather, in true Billy fashion, all but stumbles into it.

"Fuck!" is his belated response when he's already fallen on his arse, ankle twisted, hands digging into the rock and dirt beneath him. There's darkness all around with a few speckles of light between gaps in the slab and he looks behind him, through the hole he fell. Maybe two metres. Three if he's feeling wimpy. Smooth, Billy. Real fucking smooth.

He could climb back out. He's barely pushing five seven, but all he'd need to do is get a bit of a jump, a bit of leverage, a bit of *something*. Except that's why he's here, isn't it? Needed a little somethin'-somethin' and it sent him over the edge. Needs a little somethin' to fix his mess of a life. No need to get philosophical, Billy. You're on a walk. Looks like you stumbled into some old mineshaft so here's your hiccup. Always said you're up to trying new things.

"Trying New Things"

No. Too on the nose. But a good theme. Stow that away along with everything else.

So he's got two choices here. He's at the crossroads, ready for a deal with the devil (excellent titles, but he doesn't need a plagiarism lawsuit under his belt). He shrugs and decides to walk on. Dying out here would make for a good story, even if he is closing in on a decade past the 27 club. He can go out like Michael Hutchence instead, but his band better not dare keep producing.

Billy twists his backpack around to his front, unzips it, rifles through. He packed like a good boy; even looked up a provisions list on the web.

First thing he needs: torch. He takes a swig of water too, for good measure, and cringes. He never has acquired the taste after a childhood of heavy-handed cordial and soft drink swigged straight from the bottle before moving onto the harder booze. Still, he's trying to be good and if that means trading scotch for a clear liquid not of the vodka variety, so be it.

He flicks on his torch. It's a cheapie, picked up from the two-dollar shop and unlikely to last much longer than today. Bad idea? Probably, but it's what he's working with when he starts forward. Time to explore, Billy. Time to be a Big Brave Boy.

The mineshaft's bigger than he expected, and more horizontal. Billy always thought these things were meant to go straight underground; one wrong move and you're splat to the bottom. Nobody even bothering to clean you up because who wants to waste that taxpayer effort. At least that gives him the last nudge he needs to forgo fear. Billy's got nothing left to lose.

Washed up rock star who needs a thrill, and yeah, maybe he has the hots for his therapist who's sexy in that fifty-year-old-professional way but so what? Marianne flirts back. First visit and she told him how much she enjoyed his first hit, "Holidays."

That was the generic, cop-out answer. The one kind-of hit the band managed to get. A music video, a spot on Rage, a tour around Australia. Chances are Billy's therapist looked it up, found it, decided to use it as a way to build rapport. Sell-out. Only wants her dough.

Now Billy's walking and seething and thinking about how everyone's wronged him and why did he think it was a good idea to come out here instead of finding some…well, he doesn't know…yoga studio? Something hippie-dippie like that. Walking. Walking more. Humming something under his breath that might go with one of those terrible titles he's trying out when—

Shit.

He doesn't exactly fall this time, but the mineshaft changes from straight ahead to suddenly left and Billy doesn't know where he's looking but it's certainly not where he should, because his shoulder slams against it, boot twists in something, and he's stumbling all the way around.

Finally, he catches himself.

Billy's still got his torch on and waves it around. He's expecting more than what he gets, which is a hollow cavern filled with absolutely nothing. No leftover tools or piles of wood or even some rubbish dumped by squatters. It's like the whole place has been picked clean, and then Billy notices something else.

Sitting right in or close to the centre. Perfectly, specifically placed.

Billy's almost afraid to go to it, but he tells himself to stop being such an idiot and takes those needed steps. Squats down on gunshot knees and huh. What?

He's looking at a cassette tape.

He didn't even think they existed anymore. Everything digital with the odd CD or a hipster collection of vinyls. Cassettes? Billy might have some nostalgic feelings, but even he knows they had as many problems as benefits. Twisting that pencil around and around, unless the tape was too messed up, then it's a rubbish job.

All that fear is forgotten as he picks up the tape and nothing zaps him or jumps out to yell boo!

It looks new and in a thick marker are written several letters. **W I T C H 'S B R E W.** Huh.

Billy shifts the torch down a little, to the lines with the track listing. The titles are hard to read, in a cursive that looks like a drunken hand quickly jotted it down before passing out in a pile of their own sick. Some of the titles miss the premade lines entirely, going back over the one listed before it. Billy has to squint and twist and move his torch around. He thinks the light must be running out, because it all seems dimmer now. He needs to leave. Soon. Or he'll be partying by himself into the doors of doom.

" 'Trying New Things…' " He sounds out the letters, murmurs the creation of words. A hot prickling starts on the back of his neck as he gets to the next one. *Finance Guru.*

"What the fuck?" He says it like a whisper, but in a chamber this big his words echo back into his ears. A constant noise, the booming of a drum.

—*the fuck.*

*— — fuck.*

He turns the tape over, the B side. The best side. Only buying tapes as a kid when he gave the Bs a listen and deemed them worthy of his pocket money. Took them home and listened again and again and again before even thinking it worth bothering with the A-side. It's why he pushed so hard to release two-disc albums. Sold like shit, and now everything's digital and maybe that's what led to the breakdown.

Lack of B sides making him crazy. Fuck. He really is broken in the brain.

Billy re-adjusts the torch to read the writing hardly kept within the lines.

Fuck.

Fuck.

Fuck.

*Broken In the Brain* is written right there in a scrawl of black ink. Both hands shake so bad it's impossible to keep the torch steady and the words go in and out. The cassette goes in and out. Blurring like it might not even be real and Billy drops it, the clatter of an echo ringing out through the shaft.

*Hiking Through the Fucking Outback Because Your Therapist Thinks You Need Nature.*

No. No no no. Nonononono. He's hallucinating. Someone spiked his water with something, a little LSD to get this party started. A prank. A trick. A psychobabble experiment he never consented to.

"You doing this, Marianne?" he yells, voice echoing off the walls. It cuts off what he says next by coming back to himself. "You got cameras around here? Microphones?"

He gets up, not hearing those creaking knees of his that have already started giving out thanks to his lifestyle. He moves faster than he thinks he ever has, at least since being a little kid with the speed of Sonic up his sleeve. He scrambles to the walls and at first he's gentle, methodical. Looking for something that's got to be there. Then he's turning fervent. Feral. Scratching and clawing until he feels a fingernail bend backwards, snap, and keeps going. Wetness. Blood on walls. His? He feels a wire. Got the wire!

"Yes!" he screams. "Fuck! Yes!"

Billy tugs at it with all his strength and he's pulling, pulling, pulling—

*Yes! YES!*

He falls back with a gigantic oof that seems to reverberate throughout the mineshaft and beyond. Falling on his back, catching the brunt of it on two elbows that will be sore and bruised tomorrow. For now, he hardly registers any pain.

He scrambles up onto his knees and flails around for the torch and the wire, both hands convulsively roaming about. He touches something metal. Success! With all the triumphant cheer of a kid winning the school cross country race he holds it in the air.

His other hand finds the torch and he switches it back on. Good, it's working. Everything's working. Everything coming up his way and—

Billy shines the light on what he's holding and sees it's little more than some kind of root or plant vine. He drops it like it's fire. Searing his skin. A kind of frenzy takes over, his heart beating loud in his ears. An overdose in the making but there's no one here to shoot up the Narcan.

It's then he hears it.

So quiet, but it's there. Keyboard. Guitars.

And voice…voice…voice…

Billy stops his movement and holds his breath. *Shut up*, he tells his heart but of course it doesn't want to listen. The musical voice is just on the wrong side of quiet for him to make out the words and it's maddening. What are you singing? Why are you singing? *Where* are you singing?

Billy breaks into a run. It's not right and hardly even possible with his breaking-down body, but he's doing it. Slamming his body into the wood-stone walls everywhere, hitting the scaffolding somebody placed but didn't see worth bringing back out. Was it here before? Wasn't it empty?

One wrong move, Billy boy, and you're bringing the whole place tumbling down.

Question is: are you the pink piggy brother or the big, bad wolf?

Billy knows what he is. Always has. A failure. Cursed. Tried to hide it with music, with booze, with women, with moving around so much he forgets where he's from. There's roots in your feet — everyone's feet. Sometimes you can chop 'em up, but sooner or later you're forced to either find some soil or wilt and rot away. Whether or not you thrive depends on those nutrients, and there's nothing like good ol' home-grown tilling to give you the best of the best.

"Huff and puff, little piggy," he murmurs, and by now Billy knows he's insane, but he also knows it's a dog-eat-dog world out there and he's in it to win it. Embrace the insanity because it's going to get him out of here. Wherever *here* has become.

Because it's certainly not a mineshaft anymore. At least not one looking for rocks or minerals or coal or whatever the hell it once was used for. Nah, man. This place has dripping walls. Billy doesn't want to reach out and touch, but he's pretty sure it's blood. Mixed in with all the wires. Connected to all those microphones and infrared cameras that catch his movements in the dark. He swings his torch wildly and tries to catch sight, but everything's on some kind of pulley system and it swings away whenever he tries.

The music changes. Barely perceptible, but Billy's a *musician*, man. He's trained for this kind of thing. Doesn't matter that he never could pluck out a tune because he can hum it, sing it, make up rhymes on the fly. Deserves an ARIA, man, a Grammy. Needs him a placard on the Rock & Roll Hall of Fame.

It's that same slow rock beat. Something you'd have your first dance to. La-la-la-da-da-da. Something he would have picked for his own wedding if Delilah hadn't made it all her way. Honestly, Billy doesn't even remember the soundtrack only that it was all the hits of 2006 and if *that* didn't give him the first warning bells of a future divorce then it was his own stupid fault.

Another change. There's a different underlying beat to this one. Almost, *almost* pop-py but Billy decides that's because it's what he's thinking about. Cognitive bias, yeah? Hearing, seeing things because you just found them out. Buy the red car because it's unique and sexy and suddenly BAM! Everyone's got a red car. Same make and model as yours, too. Sellout.

"Not original!" he yells, his own voice bouncing back to him, but somehow the music remains at the same volume. He tries screaming. His throat raw and painful. He can still hear it, only faintly. Not enough for words but there.

Impossible to ignore.

Billy keeps moving. One step in front of the other. Sooner or later the exit will appear again and he'll haul his arse right out of here. He can't run anymore, his lungs on fire. His head pounding its own beat and he focuses on that, tries to let it consume him instead of that outside music, but it changes. Again. It *changes*. Matches that head-pounding rhythm. It's everywhere. It's consuming him. Ripping insides into outsides until he feels he might chuck. But it's louder, clearer, and for that tiny improvement he's grateful.

*When you step, when you move…*

They're not lyrics he's ever heard before, but somehow it's like his soul knows them. Like they were inside him all along and only begging to be free. Training for this. Somehow. If he wasn't so close to dying, if he wasn't so hell-bent on still moving, he'd be feeling those walls again. Sure this is all some elaborate torture technique designed by his therapist. Use Billy as the guinea pig. Sounds about right. Always the joke. The guy to kick in the arse when he's down. Why not use and abuse Billy the Great?

He's moving. Snail's pace.

*When your life's a snail's pace,*
*Don't expect more,*
*Don't expect better.*

The lyrics keep changing, the tune and the beat. It's a mess of sounds like someone's taken a mixer and gone insane at the power it offers. Press this and this and this. Turn it up, turn it down. Twist and mix the lot.

*Billy*
*Billy*
*Billy never stood a chance.*

Song or subconscious? All of it mocking.

He tries to cover his ears with his arms but they were what kept him balanced and now he's stumbling all over the place. Hit the rock. Hit the wood. Smack, bing, bam. Pinball attack.

He's in the arcade as a little kid. There's music above his favourite pinball game. Alien theme. Get it past all the little UFOs. The speaker sucks, tinny and broken and whiny if someone uses anything else electrical nearby. He feels it searing into his brain and this is it, isn't it? Somehow that pinball machine has sucked him in deep. He's the little ball while above him cackles all the rest of his bandmates. They always knew they were better than him. He was always sucking them down the drain. Spilling them like he did the booze, then licking it up off filthy hotel room floors.

DING
DING
DING

Except the bell is wrong. It's not them scoring points but instead a song starting up again. He can't hear words but he *knows* words. That makes sense, yeah? It's about pinballs. Arcades. Being smacked around by Dad and friends and cursed by the whole damn world.

Bam.
Bam.
Bam.

Billy's hitting everything but he can't feel that because he's focused on something else. Something right, right up ahead. The music gets louder until it's deafening even through his arm shield. He might as well not have skin or body anymore. He's ears and throat and chest. A scream he can't hear because the noise is deafening.

*Hiking through the fucking outback because your therapist thinks you need nature.*

This natural enough, Marianne?
Sunshine. Sunshine. Sunshine.
He's about to be free.

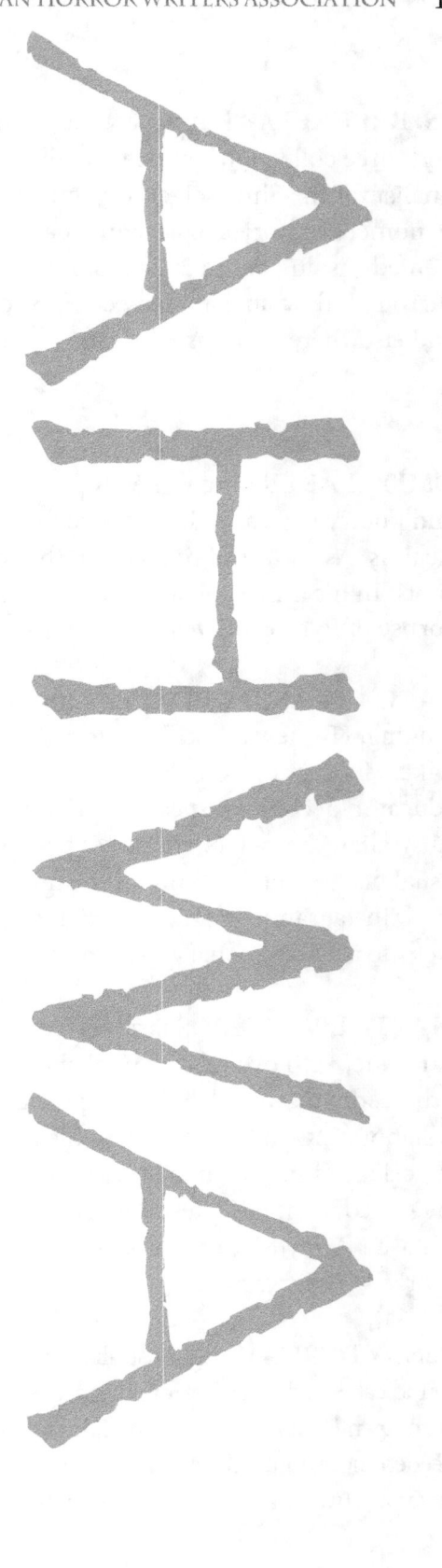

## GUEST EDITOR

**J.S. BREUKELAAR** is the award-winning American-Australian author of three novels and three collections, most recently, The Bridge and Collision: Stories, which was a finalist for the Shirley Jackson and Aurealis Awards, and Ditmar Award winner, as well as numerous stories in acclaimed anthologies and several Years Bests. Her new novella, Remedy, is due out in 2024 from PS Publishing. She lives with her family in Sydney surrounded by far too many coffee shops. You can also find her at thelivingsuitcase.com and elsewhere at @jsbreukelaar

## CONTRIBUTOR BIOGRAPHIES

**DMITRI AKERS** is a writer and poet, who lives in Adelaide (Kaurna country). His prose and poetry have appeared, or are forthcoming, in Penumbra, So It Goes, and Spectral Realms. As a lover of poetry and the weird, he wishes to draw from those intertwined roots. In his mind, the Muses' home of Parnassus shall always overlook the rotting corpse of Python at Delphi.

**ZACHARY ASHFORD** is the Aurealis-nominated author of When the Cicadas Stop Singing. His new book, The Morass: Servant of the Fly God is available through Crystal Lake. His debut novel, Polyphemus, is out through Darklit in November. He is an educator, occasional speaker, and cat-lover. His books usually feature literary themes, Australian characters, tonnes of page-turning conflict. You can buy his books in the usual places and find him on the modern hellscape we all call social media at: https://www.instagram.com/zac_ashford/ and https://www.tiktok.com/@zacharyashford8. His website is www.Zachary-ashford.com

**MATTHEW R. DAVIS** is a Shirley Jackson Award-nominated author living in Adelaide, with over eighty published short stories to his name. When not writing or procrastinating, he dabbles in spoken word, independent film, and visual design, often collaborating on the latter with his partner Meg (Red Wallflower Photography). An experienced musician, he was/is/will be bassist and vocalist for Blood Red Renaissance and icecocoon. His latest books are the Ditmar Award-shortlisted The Dark Matter of Natasha (Grey Matter Press, 2022) and the flash fiction chapbook Bites Eyes: 13 Macabre Morsels (Brain Jar Press, 2023). Find out more at matthewrdavisfiction.wordpress.com.

**PENNY DURHAM** is an Australian journalist living in Sydney (Gadigal land) with a tall man and a round cat. She's been a horror fan since reading Dracula at an inappropriate age and M.R. James lives permanently on her bedside table. Penny's the editor of The Medical Republic, a GP magazine, but needed more outlets for her spooky/silly side and began writing horror fiction in 2022. Her stories have won two awards and appeared in two anthologies, two magazines and a podcast.

**CLAIRE FITZPATRICK** is an editor and award-winning author of speculative fiction and non-fiction. She is the 2020 recipient of the Rocky Wood Memorial scholarship fund for her non-fiction anthology 'A Vindication Of Monsters – Essays on Mary Wollstonecraft and Mary Shelley' (IFWG Publishing International October 2023) and the winner of the 2017 Rocky Wood Award for Non-Fiction and Criticism. She was also nominated for the 2022 William Atheling Jr. Award for Criticism or Review. She lives in Brisbane with her husband, their fourteen animals, and two eldritch offspring. Visit her at www.clairefitzpatrick.com.au

**MASON HAWTHORNE** studied creative writing at the University of Wollongong, and has stories in Unspeakable: a Queer Gothic Anthology, The Monsters we Forgot Anthology and Kaleidoscope: A Queer Anthology 2023.

**CHLOE HERCZEG** is a sixteen-year-old college student from Canberra, Australia. Despite her young age, she has already achieved an impressive number of accomplishments. In 2019, her Sherlock Holmes story "The Adventure of a little girl's tears" was published by Belanger Books. In 2020, her picture "Banjo" was accepted into the "Black Dogs, Dark Tales" anthology published by Things in the Well, and last year (2022), her artwork "Death consumes all time" won the E.G. Harvey award at Conflux 16. Her future looks bright.

**FEBY IDRUS** is a writer, musician and arts administrator from Dunedin, New Zealand. Her work has previously been published in the Canadian horror magazine Unnerving, as well as in the New Zealand journals Headland, takahē and Hainamana. Her work was also anthologized in A Clear Dawn: New Asian Voices from Aotearoa New Zealand (Auckland University Press.) She can neither confirm nor deny that her family have had her Pākeha boyfriend for dinner.

**A.M. JOSEPH** is a writer of all things strange, dark and thrilling, with aspirations of becoming a novelist. They are an English educator based in Melbourne, Australia, currently studying a master's degree in writing. As a gay person of colour, they are passionate about LGBTQIA+ voices in fiction. You can find them on Instagram: @amjoseph.writer

**N.KING** is a biracial writer of British-Jamaican descent who lives in Sydney but still calls herself a Londoner. She has never quite outgrown her childhood fear of the things that lurk in the shadows and is particularly fascinated by psychological horror and the terror we each create for ourselves.

**CHRIS MASON** is an award-winning author who lives on Peramangk land in the Adelaide Hills of South Australia. Her stories have been published by Things in the Well, Clan Destine Press, Hungry Shadows Press, Deadset Press, and Midnight Echo. Chris is a Shirley Jackson award finalist, has won Aurealis awards for Best Horror Short Story and Best Horror Novella, and received the Australian Shadows Paul Haines award for long fiction. You can visit Chris at: facebook.com/chrismasonhorrorwriter, Threads @ thestubbypencil, or Bluesky @chrismason.bsky.social.

**BRENT MCGREGOR** hails from Australia. He lives in Sydney with his wife, daughter, and two dogs, Marvin and Otis. He likes to delve into the world of the terrifying, by writing stories that combine both the weird and the uncanny. Follow his work at brentmcgregor.com or on Twitter at @BMcGregorWrites

**LEANBH PEARSON** (she/her) lives in Canberra, Australia. An LGBTQI and disability author of horror and dark fantasy, her writing is inspired by folklore, fairytales, myth, history and climate. She's been awarded AHWA and HWA mentorships, nominated for the Ditmar Awards and winner of the HWA Diversity Grant and AHWA Robert N Stephenson Flash Fiction Story Competition. Leanbh's alter-ego is an academic in archaeology, evolution and prehistory. https://linktr.ee/leanbhpearson

**KATE POZZOBON** is a writer of shorts and novels across a variety of genres, yet always finds her way back to horror and what it can explore on the human experience. She lives in regional Victoria with her husband, daughter, and many rescued pets.

**FIONA L. RENTON,** new to the horror community, says, " Real monsters do exist. They are everyday people, and the things they are capable of are terrifying." Fiona has been writing for more than 20 years and attributes her tendency towards chilling tales to her vivid dreams. Focusing on her upcoming trilogy, Fiona writes horror in her down time to clear her head and describes her work as being chilling with a dark beauty.

**MATTHEW SCOTT** is a 31 year old writer and journalist from Whangārei and based in Auckland. In a previous life he was an English teacher in Peru, Guatemala, and Vietnam.

**EM STARR** (she/her) is an emerging Aussie horror writer, living in Melbourne on Boon Wurrung land. 2023 has been pretty good to this new kid - her short stories have appeared in anthologies and a college syllabus, and she has won and placed in several international writing comps. Get to know Em at www.emstarr.com.au

**JOSEPH TOWNSEND** is a writer of dark fiction and has previously been published in Aurealis. He resides in Brisbane.

Shirley Jackson award-winner **KAARON WARREN** has published five novels and seven short story collections. She's sold over 200 short stories to publications big and small around the world and has appeared in Ellen Datlow's Year's Best anthologies. Her novel "The Grief Hole" won all three Australian genre awards. She has lived in Melbourne, Sydney, Fiji and Canberra and her most recent book is "Bitters", a novella from Cemetery Dance. She won the inaugural AsylumFest Ghost Story Telling Competition in 2022 (the story published herein).

**PAULINE YATES** is the Australian author of Memories Don't Lie, a fast-paced science fiction novel, and the forthcoming horror short read Dream Job. An Australian Shadows Awards finalist, her short-form fiction appears in numerous publications in Australia and abroad. She's a member of the HWA and AHWA, loves writing at midnight when her muse is the most volatile, and enjoys taking pictures of the sunrise— if she wakes up in time. https://paulineyates.com/

**MEG WRIGHT** (aka Red Wallflower Photography) is a semi-professional art photographer from NSW living in Adelaide. She loves shooting urbex, live gigs, band promos, and strange environments. Her work has graced the covers of four albums and four books so far, and she illustrated the first horror collection by her partner, Matthew R. Davis. She shot a music video for Minds Untethered and is currently studying at Centre for Creative Photography. When not photographing or editing, she enjoys reading, drinking tea, and spending time with her partner and her cat, Juniper. Follow her on instagram: @red.wallflower

## CONTRIBUTOR COPYRIGHT ACKNOWLEDGEMENTS

www.ingramcontent.com/pod-product-compliance
Lightning Source LLC
Chambersburg PA
CBHW081919130726
47909CB00015B/3034